HIDING *in a*
SMALL WORLD
Nowhere to Run

HIDING *in a*
SMALL WORLD
Nowhere to Run

MELVIN PONSAK DAJI

authorHOUSE®

AuthorHouse™ UK Ltd.
1663 Liberty Drive
Bloomington, IN 47403 USA
www.authorhouse.co.uk
Phone: 0800.197.4150

Published by AuthorHouse   04/30/2014

ISBN: 978-1-4969-7811-0 (sc)
ISBN: 978-1-4969-7812-7 (hc)
ISBN: 978-1-4969-7824-0 (e)

CONTENTS

DEDICATION

This book is dedicated to God Almighty and to all youths who have resolved to shun all social vices in their societies and are committed to living purpose driven lives

ACKNOWLEDGEMENT

It is impossible to accomplish a work of this nature without the contributions of certain people. I indeed give glory to God Almighty for seeing me through this work.

Special thanks go to my lovely wife, Mrs. Juliet Akuoma Daji and our dear daughter, Miss Daniella Nanbyen Daji. I love you both so much.

My profound gratitude goes to Mr. Sunday Abbah and Pastor Stanley N. Ezinwa for reading through this book, making useful corrections and preferring priceless suggestion.

Special thanks to all who have in one way or the other supported and encouraged me while working on this book. May God bless and reward you greatly.

PREFACE

The number of youths in prisons today is increasing by the day. In fact, in most prisons there are more youths than adults. Youths, in general are inclined to breaking rules and they usually try to break away from rules and regulations at home, and even in public places. The home and society at large have not succeeded in inculcating moral, social, religious and cultural lessons in youths, as to enable them fit into the society as law abiding, disciplined and morally sound individuals.

The core objective of this book is to teach youths the value of self-discipline, vision, goal setting and commitment to their goals in life and also, to learn, from Princess' story, that the unknown future would be determined only by how each individual chooses to approach it.

Likewise, parents should find in it a lesson book on the need to raise children responsibly. If parents fail to understand how much responsibility they owe to the future of their children, the children will be left with no other option than to learn defective values from the society. Then they would usually only discover their mistakes after they find themselves in places where they ought not to have been such as prisons and rehabilitation homes. It is important to know that a person going nowhere like Princess in this book will definitely end up somewhere. Unfortunately, more often than not, the "somewhere" is an undesired place.

In this book, Princess, the main character, fortunately gets a second chance. However, some youths may not have a second chance as they may lose their lives while still on the wrong path. Youths often, do not plan to do some of the evils they are caught doing and in most cases, have only fallen victims of peer influence or pressure. Similarly, a false feeling of liberty may cause them to express their freedom beyond limits. All these have led to severe youth decadence in our society and it is becoming almost practicably impossible to redirect youths on the right path.

Princess' story in this book is worse than that of the prodigal son of the Bible, because she did not even plan to travel at all nor did she foresee that there will be a need for her to flee. She did not know what next would happen to her and she was at the mercy of circumstances. However, an evident similarity between her and the prodigal son was that, she did not die in process of going on the wrong way; she had the opportunity to return home after she was sought out from the 'hiding place' and she had 'nowhere to run'.

CHAPTER ONE

BEGINNING

Comfort of course is the desire of everyone; it is also the hope and anticipation of all in this life and even hereafter. This however is hard to come-by in Angelis town. In the hot season, one can see from a distance people sitting under shades of trees and house verandas, trying to have a good feel of the weather.

Many could be seen holding hand-fans while some others lie down in T-Shirts, but those who prefer staying in-door suffer more discomfort because the electric fans which ought to provide fresh air in the house blow hot air after working for some time. Moreover, the frequent electric power outage contributes immensely to the suffering of the people. In addition, the massive influx of flies from the Sahara further compounds the problem, creating more discomfort. People use leaves and hand-fans to chase the flies. Those who run restaurants in Angelis town also suffer in hot seasons as they always look for means of controlling the menace of millions of flies in their environment.

In the burg, animals suffer most, because no one bothers to provide them shade from the heat of the weather. They move from one place to another in search of water to drink and shade to provide for themselves coverage from the heat of the sun. Pets are not allowed to stay under shades together with people because of the flies they produce and the stench that comes out of their bodies; so only humans enjoy the most comfortable and suitable shades.

The fresh air needed by people however does not come often; this is because of the dead and still atmosphere. Leaves do not move because there is no wind to blow them; in fact, even trees need some kind of shades because they too possess some of the characteristics of humans, and when they do not get the kind of shade they need due to the excessive heat, they dry up.

The rate at which water is being consumed in the little burg is another issue worthy of note. People drink water second by seconds, minute after minutes, hour after hours. Thus water business became the most lucrative business as the demand grows higher than supply. Companies that produce water keep increasing their production level to meet up with the high demand for this essential commodity, yet hardly would a person get cold water to drink. The only available option for many is either warm or even sometimes hot water. Houses with refrigerators are no better since it is impossible to perform magic for water to get cold in the absence of steady power supply.

Mr. and Mrs. Jones's family was not exempted from this discomfort. In fact their condition seems more critical as Mr. Jones's two bedrooms were not adequate to accommodate his twelve children. The harsh weather condition sends the children scattered around looking for fresh air and shades for comfort.

Mr. Jones (as he is popularly called) was a man whose parents settled in Angelis town a long time before now. He was the eldest son of the family. He and seventeen others were born and bred in Angelis. Some of them grew up not knowing their real place of origin. Jones got married to Ketch and they gave birth to thirteen children, but one died at birth leaving twelve alive.

This family strove for survival when the sole bread winner's businesses crumbled. They suffered a lot of hardship and lived from hand to mouth. The condition then became really critical as the children grew up. Providing food, school fees, paying health services bills, providing cloths and other basic necessities became almost impossible. Those in private schools were withdrawn while a few of them were taken to public schools. Others were sent out to trade. The climax of the survival struggle was when all the children have to go out to fend for themselves. The struggle degenerated to a survival of the fittest as everyone fought hard on his or her own.

Mr. Jones's children engaged in various odd jobs for survival. Bobby, who dropped out of school at the junior school level, moved from restaurant to restaurant, washing plates and disposing refuse. That exposed him to all sort of ill and cruel ways of making ends meet. Tom, one of Jone's children joined a group of vagrants at the motor park. His activities in the park initially include motor touting, loading and offloading goods in and out of vehicles. His acquaintances which were the thugs at the park exposed him to other ills like picking pocket and stealing of passengers' luggage to the extent that police station became his regular guesthouse and subsequently, the prison became his abode.

The pride of my Jones' family is the eldest daughter who made it to the college and after graduation got a good teaching job. Thereafter she got married to a gentleman and lived happily. That was the condition of a family Princess grew up.

Her lust for material things and friends she kept greatly influenced her into learning all sorts of undesirable attitudes. Princess was quite beautiful; she always looked gaiety and never dreary. Her glamour attracted men and women alike. Whenever she dresses properly, creatures stumble. Initially her beauty opened a way for her to make ends meet, as men trooped in and out after her like vultures gathering around carcass.

Princess Belinda Jones, the seventh child of Mr. Jones began he incredible career with minor stealing whenever she was in need. At very tender age in the kindergarten, she would steal other pupil's food anytime she had the opportunity. If caught, and asked why she did that, she always say, I am hungry. It got to the point that the school authorities wrote a letter to Mr. Jones blaming him for his inability to provide adequate food for his daughter and he was admonished to do something about Princess's bad behaviour immediately before it becomes too late. Being a poor man who was only trying to make ends meet for a large family, keeping his children under control became a major problem for him.

Princess's mother couldn't make any positive impact as some of the children grew older. She was the quiet type. She would not harm even a fly. She disliked fracas. She appears responsible but she was actually irresponsible when it comes to training her children. Because she wouldn't want to hurt her children, most of them did not give her the desired respect she deserved. Her frequent noise in the house at times sounds like un-quantized music. She was more often than not seen as being frivolous. All she did was to watch her children in silence as if the house was outside her jurisdiction as a mother.

Princess dropped out of school when she was in her senior secondary class at the high school. She could not cope with embarrassments she received as a result of her dubious activities in the school, ranging from stealing, fighting, duping and sneaking out of school to immoral acts and disobedience to authority. The degree of her activities shortly before she left school revealed that she would be in trouble sooner or later if she was not called to order and totally reformed. Unfortunately, things rather got worse.

Her troubles began when a group of advanced vagrants and vagabonds organized a jamboree at a certain period, and Princess and three of her closest friends sneaked out of school for the party. The venue was in a bush as far off as half a kilometer from the nearest building in the town. There, they cleared the bush and made a large tent for the celebration. The rules for the party as stated in the invitation cards were, that admission was strictly for couples only and the dress code was 'You know'. There would be no admission without invitation and by implication a boy or girl could not go to the party alone. Two persons of opposite sex must go together and for the dressing, a girl must wear particular dresses such as mini skirt or body hug or any sleeveless clothes that at least exposes the body, while for the boys at least any kind of 'raster jeans'. Decent and corporate dressing was totally prohibited.

At the camp, no non-alcoholic drink was allowed. Therefore all sorts of alcoholic drinks and cigarettes including hem were displayed for the parkers on a platter of gold. They drank, smoke and danced the hell out of themselves.

Some danced wildly, some engaged in all sorts of sexual immoralities and some in their dead-drunk state dosed. The party which started at about 12:00 midnight reached its climax at 3:00 am when everyone was totally wild.

Suddenly, there was a hullabaloo outside the tent of the camp; what was it? Fighting? Princess had sneaked out of the tent to meet a guy who had admired her earlier. He passed a note to her saying that she should meet him at the back of the tent at a specific time. As soon as Princess went out to meet him, they disappeared into the bush and came back after about an hour. Moray who had been running helter skater, looking for her was at this time, leaning on a car, smoking his marijuana as usual. On sighting Princess, Moray never waited for an explanation; he rushed at both of them with a heavy slap on Princess's face and a bottle on the guy's head. There was a hubbub at the scene which later metamorphosed into a free-for-all fight. Weapon such as broken bottles, stones, stick and guns were freely used. In the end, cars windscreens were smashed, many were wounded and a person killed. Princess and her friends in the process parted ways, running for their dear lives.

The following day, police began arrest as investigation continued. Princess was nowhere to be found. The police went to her school on several occasions to apprehend her but their several visit and search for her was to no avail. Her parents' house was also searched as well as that of some of her relations. Princess' friends searched all the possible places she could be found but all their effort was in vain.

The mysterious disappearance of Princess became the talk of the town. Everybody already knew her capability coupled with the fact that such disappearance was not the first of its kind. Princess' father said. "I can recall vividly, about a year ago, Princess left home and never returned. All efforts to get her proved abortive. That was reported to the police and announced by the media. We were thrown into great confusion and panic. I prayed to God for help. Then one evening, I was resting outside and she walked into the house confidently as if nothing has happened. 'Good evening Daddy' she greeted and I was furious at her. I picked an electric cable and gave her a beating of her life. No one came to her rescue in the house because all were as well tired of her bad attitudes. After the beating we began to converse.

"Princess, where are you coming from? I asked. She was mute.

'I said, where are you coming from?' She was quiet.

5

'Are you deaf? Let this be the last time; Princess, where have you been?'

'To Zima', she responded.

'Who do you know and what business or mission do you have in Zima?

'My friend's elder brother's wedding . . .'

What! You left my house for three weeks and you are now telling me you attended your friend's elder brother's wedding? How many days did it take to conduct a wedding?

'One' she answered.

Why was your friend's elder brother's three weeks? Upon whose consent did you go? Ehm I . . .'

'Shut up you liar! Tell me the truth or I kill you today'

Princess refused to tell the truth despite all efforts to make her talk. I got angry and stood up. I again asked her to tell me the truth but she refused. Her refusal made me furious and I booted her. She fell and fainted. I left her there. Her sister took her to the clinic. On return, I called her and talked to her. 'You are a girl today; tomorrow you would be a woman and a mother. I'm sure you will not be happy to see what you are doing now being done by your children. Why can't you be obedient, respectful and responsible? No man will marry a girl with dirty habits as yours. You better change before it becomes too late. Your education is very important as well. You have to compose yourself and work hard. God will surely crown your effort and you will have a successful future with a good husband and happy children.

'Thank you Dad, I am very sorry and I promised this will never happen again' Princess replied.

Well I have handed her over to God. If God does not rescue her, what can I, a mortal man do?"

Who is to blame for Princess' delinquency, Jones, God or Princess herself? A Biblical injunction states: Train up a child in the way he should go and when he is old he will not depart from it. Mr. and Mrs. Jones lived a life of liberality. Quest for money was their utmost priority. Before Mr. Jones' business crumbled, he used to leave home early in the morning, at times before his children woke up and he returns home when they were already sleeping. He sometimes spent between three to six days or more outside on business engagements.

Mrs. Jones on the other hand had her business to manage—she gave little or no attention to her house and children's behaviour. She woke up every morning only to instruct the eldest of her daughters to ensure that the little ones ate their breakfast before they go to school and to prepare lunch for them after school.

Children were left each day with absolute liberty at home. Everyone was free to do whatever they feel they should do and even after school when Mum and Dad were around, there was no difference. The older ones never exhibited good examples to the younger one—they did whatever they wished. At no time did this family of fourteen ever gathered to pray or discuss family matter. The children were never shown the way to behave in proper manner as there was no absolute parental care and rule over them. The older children correct the younger ones when they do wrong while they (older ones) had no one to correct them when they do wrong.

Jones' house was characterized by violence, indiscipline, ruthlessness, hatred, quarrels and irresponsibility. Children would struggle for food at meal times—injure themselves. The older ones sometimes took the lion share, leaving the younger ones in tears. Washing soap in the house and other toiletries were not equally shared. Some of the children pack and hide them so that when there was want of them, they would have to themselves. Besides this, some of the children steal food stuffs at home to cook in their friend's house because of the dissatisfaction they put up with the little meal offered to them at home. It is taking risk keeping money at home because it will soon disappear. Disrespect was at its peak in Jones' house; especially in the older children who felt they have grown old and should enjoy their due independence. No one dared warn or talk to the other; 'mind your business' was the policy in the house. The whole affairs of the house always culminate into clash of titans and by implication, survival of the fittest.

Mr. Jones realized at a point that it was almost too late to control his children. They were used to such a harsh pattern for a long time and it was difficult, almost impossible to bring them back to track. At the collapse of his business, he began to stay at home. That was the period he began to really see his children's acts of indiscipline and irresponsibility. Mr. Jones tried his best to correct their behaviour at that time but it seemed not possible because most of them were already entangled in it. He would gather and speak to them, threatening to punish anyone who misbehaved, but his warning fell on deaf ears, because of the level of their involvements in various acts of indiscipline. He sometimes felt like leaving the house because of disturbances. But will he run away from home because of his children? He would asked himself.

The Jones began to think of God when the problem was getting out of hand. They met for the first time as a family for devotion. He began serious prayers for his children, business and God's mercy hoping that things would change for the better.

Chapter Two

MIGRATION

How possible is it to believe that a person disappeared into thin air? After all the law of gravity states that whatever goes up must come down. Could Princess have gone to another planet? What then is the mystery behind her disappearance?

The world seemed larger than its normal size for Princess. Trees of the forest could not contain her. She felt the mountains could help but none came at all. The thought of the ocean worsened the situation as its imaginary waves contributed immensely in aggravating her fears. If it were possible, she would ascend into the sky and probably hide herself behind the clouds, but God never gave her the grace of ascending up there. Princess also must have wished the ground could open so that she could go down into it and hide herself and take refuge there; but that was not possible.

Princess ran towards an unknown direction that night after the fight at party. As she ran, the bush became quite and quieter. Sounds of birds and wind did not make her afraid as she was under the influence of alcohol. When she got to a nearby stream, (already fatigued) she sat down under a baobab tree and slept off.

The ray of the sun woke Princess up in the morning. She wondered where she was.

"Where am I?" Princess soliloquized.

"Who brought me here?"

"Where are my shoes and bag?"

"Why am I not at home?"

She sat down and began to weep with fear. It was like a dream. She began to recall what happened the previous day. She recalled that she was at a party when fight broke out but she could not remember the rest accounts after the fight.

"I will go home" Princess thought to herself. So she got up and began to walk towards an unknown direction. On the way she met a woman and her daughter gathering firewood.

"Good morning madam" said Princess

"Good morning my daughter" she replied.

"Please, can you show me the way out of this place?" She requested the woman.

"How did you get to this place?" the woman asked.

"I don't know" Princess answered.

"Oh! So you are one of them?" The woman interrupted, pointing a finger at Princess.

"No I I was only there and . . ."

"Well, young girl, that's the road", the woman said, pointing towards the direction.

'The police are there looking for you". She informed Princess.

"What! Police!" Princess exclaimed. 'Please ma, are the police arresting?

'They were here some minutes ago. They have arrested some people". The woman answered.

Princess on hearing that, stood, unable to move for a moment because of the fear that gripped her. She became nervous, knowing very well that she was instrumental to the cause of the fight at the party, which resulted in the fellow's death.

As the woman continued gathering her fire wood, Princess walked back with great feeling of despondent. She felt prison would be her home the moment she was caught. Princess was sure that if she is caught nothing under the sun would save her from the hands of the law.

'How long will I stay in Jail? Five years, ten years or life imprisonment—God forbid! I will not be caught. Yes, no one will ever apprehend me! She assured herself with great hardihood. She made up her mind to escape at all cost, even if it would cost her the last drop of blood in her body. She began to move toward the opposite direction; filled with panic, she always look back as she moved alone through the bush. Whenever she heard any sound or even if it was an unusual sound of a bird, she looked back thinking that the police were probably close.

She trekked for about five hours and became tired. There was neither water nor food to eat. She looked at the sky but no help came. Prayer to her would be void considering the gravity of her offence and sin. Princess thought nature seemed to be against her that moment, as no river provided water for her. The trees in the bush could not give her fruit to eat. To worsen the situation, the sun became hostile and caused her great discomfort as if it was particularly angry with her or perhaps punishing her for her sins. In the midst of the trees in the bush, the only favour Princess got was music made by birds. If it were possible, she wished, she could communicate with the birds; probably she would get her immediate needs—water and food. But anytime she got close to them, they always fly away.

The journey continued until sunset. When princess got to a small hill, all attempts to climb it proved abortive because she was very hungry and tired altogether. She decided to lie down under a tree till day break.

At sunrise, Princess woke up and received salutation from the birds who were now her friends. She sat down and reflected over that excruciating situation. Very hungry, thirsty and dirty, she began to ascend the hill gradually and finally made it to the apex. After sometime, she heard a husky voice. As she jumped up, two men surrounded her with knives and machetes.

"Who are you?" They asked.

"I-I-I am . . ."

"Who and what brought you here?"

"I I missed my way". She answered.

For climbing the sacred hill and touching the sacred stone, we shall take you to the shrine priest to consult the gods before calamity befalls us in our village, the men concluded.

Princess began to cry when she heard that. The men took her to the shrine where she was kept in a cage meant for captives. According to their tradition, it was a sacrilege for a man who is not initiated or a woman of whatsoever caliber to go near that stone. The hill was called "The hill of sacrifice" because that was the only place for sacrifice in that village. Sacrifices done in other places were regarded as abomination and therefore not acceptable to the gods. That made the hill so sacred to the people. The shrine that Princess was taken to is known as the "Death Temple". From history, anyone taken to that shrine will never return again. No man except the menservants of the Shrine priest was allowed to go and come out unhurt.

Princess thought that was the end of the road for her. The priest's verdict on her was that she would be sacrificed on the sacred stone at exactly the same time she was caught after six months of purification.

In the first two weeks of purification, Princess was fed with water mixed with corn flour. Her new diet was not pleasant and good for human consumption, but she had no choice but to eat in order to stay alive. No one ever talked with her as she underwent the purification. Anytime food was brought, they would quietly open the cage and drop it without a word. She dared not ask for water or any additional food. Princess's diet changed after a while to pumpkin without salt. She was subsequently served several traditional foods as required for purification.

One evening, a servant brought some food to Princess, and as the rule applied, it was a taboo for any servant to talk to any person undergoing purification. Touching a person in the process of purification attracts instant death. Unknown to the servant, Princess had planned that whenever a servant brings food, she would grab him and asphyxiate him; then escape. Princess pretended to be sleeping close to the door and as soon as the servant opened the door and dropped the first calabash and turned to bring in the second, Princess held his left hand and pulled him in with all the strength in her in order to strangulate him; but the servant overpowered her and ran out of the cage.

Foolish enough, the man ran away leaving the cage opened; not because she was stronger than him but because he had touched an abominable 'object' which the penalty is death. To save him from death he must put ashes all over his body and show himself to the priest who will consult the gods to know whether he should be purified or killed.

Princess escaped towards the opposite direction in the process. She ran as she had never done before.

On hearing the report of the servant, the warning drum was sounded, accompanied by the bullhorn. Women all over the village began to weep. Those cooking brought down their pots and quenched the fire. They all gathered at the village square. All men ran to the Priest's shrine to know what had happened. The people were so disturbed on hearing the warning drum that was sounded. Why the horn today? Everybody wondered. The men gathered at the shrine, each with dust on his forehead. The Priest who dressed up in lion skin, addressed the people:

'My people, we are in great trouble. The strange lamb to be sacrificed has escaped. She touched Ibechi, the god's faithful servant. What a sacrilege! The gods have given us two options, to search for her and bring her back to be sacrificed on the hill of sacrifice or we will sacrifice three virgins amongst us. This must be done within twenty-four hours else, calamity will befall our dear village. Go to the four corners of the earth—North to

South, East and West and get her back dead or alive. I said get her back! The chief hunter will head the search. Go! The gods be with you'.

Princess became conscious as she ran. She moved with gumption in order to avoid falling into the hands of her seekers. After hours of intense running, and walking, she came to a stream. There she sat down looking worried. She was afraid of going into the stream to drink of its water and probably take her bath. She moved closer and listened carefully to waves of the water. She became more afraid because the whole place was completely dark. Since princes was not sure of another stream ahead and being afraid of the available one, she decided to stay near the stream till day break in order to have a drink and take her bath. Unable to sleep, she lay down under a tree, thinking about the past events. She thought it would have been better in prison than being a sacrificial lamb. She imagined the cage in the shrine—it was almost a dungeon. One could not differentiate between night and day in there. The place stunk as it was the toilet as well as bedroom. That was the least place she had ever dreamt of being in. At least, the prison was paradise compared to the cage in the shrine. In the case of a prison, a person would be set free after completing his or her jail term, but in the cage, there is no hope of freedom forever. No hope to all who get into the hands of those primitive captors.

The damsel woke up in the morning at sunrise and she walked to a mahogany tree and climbed it. She looked round and saw no sign of any living creature. She then came down and went to the stream. She first of all touched the water; it looked clean and pleasant to the eyes, so she drank of it and swam in the water for a short while. That was the first time Princess had her bath after three months since she was a captive. There was no container for her to reserve water for future use, so she drank enough and took off again.

Along the way in the bush, Princess saw a baobab tree with few fruits on it. She tried to climb but could not, because of the size of the tree. She tried to pluck the baobab fruit with stone but she couldn't. She looked for sticks and began to throw at the fruits. The first two sticks hung on the tree. It was the fourth stick that brought down a baobab fruit. Princess sat down under the tree, broke the fruit and began to lick, after which she rested for a while then continued her journey again.

Towards evening, she came to a footpath. From a distance, she saw men, women and children carrying sacks, basin and all sorts of containers, moving towards a direction. From all indication, one can presume that they were coming from a market. Princess became afraid of joining them since she didn't know where they were going. 'Let it not be that they are from the village from where I escaped', she thought within herself. Then she thought again, by the way, the village is too far from here. So she encouraged herself and moved closer to the road and sat down on a stone and watched people passing. As she looked, two girls who seemed to be of her peer surfaced. Princes immediately squeezed her face until tears came out; she jumped out of the bush shouting: 'Help! Help!!'

One of the girls dropped the bag she was carrying and wanted to run but the other called her back.

"What happened?" the lady asked.

"They wanted to kill me" Princess answered.

"Who?"

"Some people."

"Are they still there?" the lady asked.

"No, they have run away" she replied.

"It's alright, stop crying" one of the girls said.

"Where are you from?" one of the damsels inquired.

"I—I, don't know. I'm lost". Princess again busted into tears.

"Don't worry; would you come with us to our home?" Princess nodded her head in response.

The three girls walked down the narrow path for about thirty minutes and they got to the house somewhere at the outskirt of the burg situated on a highland.

At home, Princess' new friends served her food which she ate within a short time. They gave her water and she took her bath. Her friends gave her new sets of cloths. That was when Princess changed the clothe she wore to the party three months earlier. She felt relieved and uplifted. She relaxed on a chair as she looked round the room.

"So, what is your name?" one of the girls asked.

"Vera", Princess lied.

"Where are you from?" the girls asked.

At that question, Princess was speechless.

"Where do your parents reside?" one of the girls asked sympathetically.

Princess began her fictitious fabricated story with crocodile tears rolling down her face and water-like mucous running down her nostrils. "I have no father or mother; I grew up as an orphan. I was only told that my father died when my mother was pregnant and my mother died also immediately she gave birth to me. I survived through the help of a woman who offered to assist me. When I was growing up she became so ferocious to me, I became the working machine of the house as well as the scapegoat for all offences committed by her children and I . . ."

Princess burst into tears again. The girls moved closer to her with compassion—one of them put her arm around her shoulder and they comforted her not to weep anymore.

"I kept on enduring, (Princess continued) . . . until a time came when I beat her child who failed to do a little work I assigned him to do. The woman came back that evening and was so angry with me. She rained on me all the insults one can ever think of on earth and . . ." Princess cleared her throat and wiped her face, and then she continued:

". . . she told me to pack my things and leave her house. She also threatened that if I did not leave within ten minutes, she would throw me out. I begged her but she pushed me out and threw my things out afterward. I slept in the rain that night. I tried to beg her the following day but she threatened to pour hot water on my face if I dare show my feet at her door step anymore".

"Oh! Human beings are wicked," one of the girls exclaimed with tears all over her face.

"I left the house that fateful day thinking that I would find rest but it was as if I was thrown into a deeper pit when I encountered with men of the underworld who wanted to use me for ritual"

"What!" one of the girls exclaimed. I narrowly escaped in the bush. It was just that God loves me so much and He wanted me to live, otherwise I would have been forgotten by now."

The girls sat still for about a minute.

"Oh dear Vera, I'm sorry for all that happened" said one of the girls.

"That will not happen again," said the other.

"You will stay with us here; we are your parents, brothers and sister." the other girl added.

Princess' eye brightened because that was what she wanted and she achieved it by her tricks.

"My name is Benny" one of the damsels said.

"Queen is my name," said the other

"This house is now for Queen, Vera and Benny—be comfortable, feel at home and enjoy yourself". Queen said.

Princess became happy as she finally got a place of rest. After all the police would not locate her; and as for her parents, that wasn't her business anymore. As far as Princess was concerned, if they like they can go to hell.

The first night Benny went out and never returned till the following morning. In the evening, Benny, Queen and Princess went out for sight-seeing to get Princess acquainted with the town. She was shown the church where Queen and Benny attended once in a blue moon. She admired the wonderful building with flowers planted and stones arranged in rows. The Area Court and the police out-post were also shown to Princess. They also went to the stream, which served as the major source of water supply to the burg, the town's market square, primary and community secondary school, the cottage hospital which served about seven villages and a lot of other places. When Princess became tired, the girls went back home for a rest.

Within three weeks, Princess noticed that none of her cronies was gainfully working anywhere but they lived averagely alright. All she noticed was the regular influx of men at different intervals. They were always introduced as friends and uncles.

It never occurred to Princess that her friends were prostitutes, until a time when they began to show her their trade.

"Queen," Princess called one night. "It's almost twelve midnight and Benny is not yet back. Isn't she coming back?"

"No," Queen responded.

"But at times you also spent days outside."

"Yes, I'm sure it's not new to you." Queen answered.

"What do you mean? do you have another house elsewhere or . . . ?"

"Look my dear," Queen interrupted, "You will get to understand with time. Life is all about survival; all a man or woman does on this planet earth is for the sole aim of survival. We are staying in Koke town like birds of the air; we have to strife for survival and . . ."

"You mean you are prostitutes?" Princess interrupted.

"It's not prostitution but a means of livelihood."

"Aren't you girls afraid of AIDS?" Princess asked.

"Hey Princess, it's about time we slept"

"Just suspend that topic . . ."

Queen entered her blanket, leaving Princess with her eyes wide open.

"Does it mean that Queen and Benny are prostitutes?" Princess thought. "Does it mean that I will join them if I must stay with them? How possible? I can't. But will I continue to be a dependent? No! I will get a job somewhere. What kind of job and where? What if they attempt to introduce me into it? My refusal might make them send me packing, and that would mean another trouble for me. But what if I agree? Would that make me the worst sinner on earth? God knows my situation and so he should understand. Well, if they insist that I must join them, what option do I have, being a parasite?" Princess kept on soliloquizing until she slept off.

Later, Queen and Benny introduced Princess deeply into prostitution. She began to go out at night and return the following morning. Initially, she would go out with her friends as she was new to the trade. But when Princess got initiated and became an expert, she would spend three days before coming back home. Whenever they meet after 'business,' they would gather together and discuss how it went—they talked about who make the biggest catch and then about future connections, if any. They would buy lots of things and make merry. At times they drink to stupor.

Pregnancy was never a threat to their profession. They had an herbalist in a nearby hamlet who gave them concoction on monthly basis to prevent pregnancy as long as they fulfilled their part of the deal by bringing returns due for him. Each time they fulfill their obligation, he tells them 'Go my daughters. The sky is your limit.'

The three girls in furtherance of their trade sometimes clash over men. Whatsoever it was, it did not matter as far as money comes out of it. It was strictly business and nothing else. Queen's "uncle" (as they called their customers) came one day whilst she had gone out with another man. Princess went out with him instead and after that Princess and Queen later discussed their experiences with him and laughed over it. They nicknamed their customers "Toys." The name is usually called in their absence.

After three years of promiscuity, Princess got into trouble bigger than the one she ran away from. On that fateful night, Benny's 'toy' came to the house with an albino, a contractor from the city. He was simply introduced as Vann.

Vann picked Princess to keep him company throughout his stay in that burg. Princess stayed with her albino client in a hotel for three days. On the last day when he was about leaving, he opened his briefcase and dropped a bundle of money on the bed where Princess was lying down.

"That is your money." Vann said.

"How much?"

"Count and see."

Princess counted the money and hissed.

"Mr. Vann or whatever you call yourself, this money is just for one night. You still have two bundles to drop."

"Hey girl, don't be silly. That money is enough for you." Vann said.

"See Mr. Man, if you want us to leave this hotel peacefully, you better pay my money correctly." Princess said, with her countenance showing that she was not joking.

The man picked his briefcase and said, 'If you don't want to go, well, you can remain in the hotel but as for me, I have important business to attend to, so you either pick the money or leave it.' Princess jumped out of bed.

"What did you say? I will never let you go unless you pay my money in full."

When Vann discovered that Princess was serious, he brought out another bundle of money, divided it into two and handed it over to Princess.

"Look" Princess said. "I will not accept three bundles if one note is removed talk less of one and a half. After all, you kept me here for three consecutive nights and you think you will go free?"

Vann became angry and wanted to walk out, so Princess quickly ran to the door and got hold of the key. In an attempt to forcefully get the key, Vann hit Princess on the stomach. It culminated into a serious fight and the room became boisterous. Vann forcefully took the key and as soon as he turned towards the door, Princess took two bottles of beer near the bed and simultaneously hit him with both on the head. The man managed to turn back probably to revenge but he slumped and lay in the pool of his own blood. Princess began to shiver. Her worry was that she was in for another trouble which will involve the police again.

Princess picked the money on the bed, opened the door quietly and locked it behind her. She removed the key and left with it. She ran home where she met Queen and Benny waiting to celebrate the big catch.

"'Should I tell my friends?" Princess thought. "No, they may delay me. I can't even trust them because they may betray me." Princess went straight to the room, opened her box, picked all the money and came out. She didn't pick any other thing to avoid suspicion.

"What's wrong?" Benny asked.

"Nothing, I just have to rush to see Vann before he leaves finally."

"Hasn't he paid you?"

"Yes." Princess answered.

"Ah, you better hurry up right now before he gets away." Queen said.

"I will be back soon" Princess said.

"Make sure you bring goodies" Benny said, laughing.

"Like what?" Princess asked.

"Juice, my kind of wine . . ."

"And that kind of meat you bought the other day"

"Just wait for me; I will bring all those things."

"Good" the girls shouted as they wished Princess Good-bye.

Unknown to them, Princess was actually running away finally. She went to the bus station and boarded a bus to the city.

CHAPTER THREE

ANOTHER MISERY

Princess sat on the rear seat of the bus as it accelerated out of Koke Town. The vehicle was not as fast as Princess wanted. She wished the bus could fly so she could get out of Koke as quick as possible, but her wish was thwarted by frequent mechanical faults of the bus for which reason the driver has to stop again and again. Any time the bus stopped due to a fault Princess would dash into the bush where no one passing could see her until the driver invites them back into the bus.

The stoppage that made her panic the most was when the bus front tire punctured. While the driver was fixing the spare tire, a bus coming from Koke stopped close by and in it was a policeman. Princess walked briskly into the bush. She thought the news of her crime and escape has broken and that the police were after her. But the policeman was on a private mission and the bus driver only stopped to see if there was any help he could offer.

The bus arrived at the city in the evening and everyone alighted and walked towards different directions. Princess had no specific direction to go, thus she stood still watching people dismissing. In a valley of indecision, Princess stood for about thirty minutes. Later she began to move towards a direction. Some meters away, she saw buses loading in preparation for night journey.

'My safety is not guaranteed here' Princess said to herself. 'I better join another bus to the farthest destination so that my whereabouts may not be known. As she moved towards the vehicles, she saw a canteen ahead of her with many people eating there. Princess went in and joins the queue with her plate. When she was served, she went and sat in an isolated angle and a young man sitting very close to her stood up and was about to leave.

"Excuse me please", Princess called to the man.

"Yes, how may I help you?" the man asked.

"Em yes, where are those buses going?"

"The guy named various destinations."

"Are you also traveling?" Princess inquired.

"Of course, yes."

"To where, please?"

"Kirma City."

Princess went to the bus immediately after her meal and she obtained the ticket to Kirma after verifying that Kirma was a very far distance.

The journey, which commenced late evening, continued uninterrupted for hours until about two o'clock in the morning when robbers attacked the bus. The bus was moving at a high speed that morning when the driver noticed a trap ahead. The robbers used a very long plank, fixed sharp nails all over it and nailed both ends of the plank at both side of the road. The robbers stationed about a hundred and twenty meters away from where they nailed the plank. At that point, the robbers used a trailer truck, which they robbed earlier on to block the road.

The driver who was moving at a high speed applied brake when he noticed the trap, but could not stop instantly, and as a result, he ran into the trap. The bus tires were punctured. The driver, knowing that he was in danger, (though there was no sound of gunshot) kept on moving under a mistaken belief that he has escaped. Just few meters ahead he saw the roadblock. This time around it dawned on him that there was no way out, so he decelerated and stopped. The armed men, numbering about twenty, came out and surrounded the bus. Three of the terribly looking masked robbers got into the bus. One stood at the door while two went to the rear.

"Hey! Everybody hands up" commanded one of the gang members in a husky voice.

"We are here for serious business. No one should take us for granted, for we are not here for jokes. We will 'waste' anyone who dare waste a second out of our limited time. Now let me show you an example to proof how serious we are" He walked about six steps into the bus and picked a young man up and shot him in the forehead. "The same will happen to anyone who dare misbehave. You will go out one after the other with your entire valuables. Surrender them at the door and you'll be shown where to lie down. Failure to comply with this instruction means losing your life. Therefore, choose you this day which you would prefer, your life or your properties?"

The robbers collected their money, all valuables and belongings then they left. Some of the passengers were severely beaten and wounded because they had little or no money at all. One man was killed because he told the robbers he had transferred his money earlier that morning via a bank, so that when he arrives at his destination he might withdraw it.

"Since you don't want us to get your money, you will not live to enjoy it as well," said one of the bandits pointing a gun at the man's face.

They shot him twice in the head despite all pleas.

He died instantly.

After the robbery, the perpetrators of the crime got into their car and zoomed off. Many after the incident burst into tears; others looked round to see what was left in their luggage.

Princess cried and cried because the whole money she had was robbed of her in that process—she was in a fix. She cried and rolled on the ground. Even when other passengers offered to give her free condoling services, she refused to be comforted.

In the morning the police was informed about the robbery and they went to the scene of the incident, took statements and did all the formalities after which they assisted the passengers to Kirma.

Princess was not herself when she alighted in Kirma. With the trauma of the previous day's event, she was thrown into great confusion.

"Where do I start?" Princess soliloquized.

"I know no one here and I have no money. What do I do? Where do I spend the night?" Princess reflected as she sat down at the bus station. She was very hungry but there was no food to eat.

After a second thought, she considered going to a hotel to get a man who would pick her for the night. Probably that would help her get money to start life all over. At about nine o'clock that evening she went to Liberty Boulevard and sat close to a hotel, making observation with expectations. About an hour later Princess noticed that there was no sign of her usual trade.

"May be it is too early" she thought as she waited for two more hours, but nothing seems to be happening. At about midnight, Princess walked into the hotel confidently. She saw people drinking, playing different games and various activities going on. That proved Princess' initial thought wrong, because she thought earlier that it was a local hotel. The environment was beautified with flowers and trees. There was a set of cars parked by the right entrance through the main gate. Adjacent to the park was a swimming pool and just by it was the picnic camp. By the left was the road leading to the restaurant and bar. Just before the bar was an indoor sport hall. The hall looked bright and clean. Security men could be seen all over the hotel premises in well-ironed black and white uniform.

"What a beautiful environment!" she exclaimed. "It seems this hotel is for the bourgeois." Princess thought it would be easier for a bourgeois to pick her for the night to enable her make money but she was disappointed when the security men threw her out for wandering aimlessly in the hotel.

She left the hotel premises that night at about one o'clock. As she was walking along the street, a vehicle came from behind her and stopped. Princess felt a relief, thinking a prospective customer had come to pick her. Two men in uniform alighted from the van. The hotel boulevard had been a place where policemen checked regularly because it served as a place for prostitutes and a stronghold of robbers. Robbers used to attack people coming out of the hotel, so, prostitutes stopped going there because the police had threatened to deal with anyone caught there at night.

"Who are you?"

'I I'm Nana," Princess lied.

"What are you doing outside at this hour of the day?"

Princess stood still without a word. Later she tried to speak but could not convince the policemen. After series of questioning they discovered that Princess was disingenuous in her statements. She told them that she was from a far journey. She was subsequently arrested.

At the police station that afternoon, a girl of Princess' age was brought in and detained in the same cell with Princess.

"Hello sister. How are you?" Princess greeted.

"I'm fine," said the girl looking at princess.

"I'm sorry for asking but please how did you get here?' Princess asked.

'Just forget, my sister. It was a foolish friend of mine who wanted to play over my intelligence and I showed her that no woman born of another woman can intimidate me'.

"A y-a-a! Sorry," Princess sympathized.

"What is your name?" The girl asked.

'I'm Nana,' Princess responded.

"Wow! That's wonderful! I have an old time friend whose name is Nana. In fact we were so intimate. I remember we used to eat, sleep and do other things together until we later parted."

"Well, that's life for you," said Princess. 'And what's your own name?'

"Oh sorry my dear, my name is Anita. My middle name is

Francisca but it is very silent.

I'm popularly known as Anny Babe"

"That's a sweet name,' said Princess as she smiled.

"But what is the meaning of Anita?"

"Anita means mercy."

". . . and Francisca?"

"Francisca is a German name meaning freedom,"

Anita said, raising up her two hands.

"So you mean you are a free person?'

"Of course, yes! The world is a free place, so everyone has to live his or her life as it pleases him, as long as he or she does not infringe on another's right."

"But if you are really free, why are you now confined in this police cell?"

"Hey, I told you before that it was just a little quarrel between me and a friend . . ."

"That means your freedom on earth is restricted; especially now that you are in police custody."

"That I know, but I will soon be out."

"When you get out, remember me, please."

"Why not?" Anny said.

"So can I now call you miss Freedom, right?"

"Yes of course I like that," Anny said, laughing.

Anny was invited later to the investigating police officer's office and as she went, Princess began to give a second thought to their discussion; she thought that her second name Belinda means a little serpent and a serpent was always out to destroy. Could that be the reason for her problems? But does a name really matter? She pondered. What difference does it make if someone bears the name 'God' and another 'Devil'. 'I don't think there is any problem? I feel a name is just for identification and that's all, Princess concluded.

As soon as Anny returned, she told Princess that she would be released soon. Princess' heart skipped.

'Why were you brought here?' Anita asked. 'It is a long story my sister. I was travelling to this city to settle down for a business or probably look for a job, when armed robbers attacked us and collected all we had. We narrowly escaped death. Since I have no money to spend the night in a hotel, I felt I could just sleep by the roadside but as I was standing somewhere along the street . . .' tears rolled down her eyes as she spoke. "The . . . the police came and arrested me. Now I have nobody in this town. I know nobody and I don't know what to do." Princess concluded crying aloud.

Anny was greatly touched by princess' story and she promised to help. By the way, she has initially thought of inviting Princess to her home, and now, Princess' story has given her a good opportunity to give her the invitation.

After Anita's freedom, she worked out Princess' release and they went home together.

"Welcome to my humble abode" Anny said.

"Thanks." Princess answered.

"This house henceforth is not mine alone, but ours." Anita said straight into Princess' eyes.

"You are free to go inside and see things for yourself. I will make you comfortable! Your happiness is my utmost priority. I want you to experience real peace and enjoy yourself all through. When a lawyer says, 'res ipsa loquitur', it means, the fact speaks for itself. Now I want you to just relax, the fact will speak for itself." Anita assured Princess.

Princess was carried away by Anita's sentimental talks. Anita came and hugged her, led her to the chair and they sat down.

Princess looked round the room—it was a beautiful setting. The two-room self-contained apartment was so beautifully decorated with flowers and assorted souvenirs.

Anita took Princess to the bathroom.

'What a nice place!' Princess exclaimed.

It was very neat with tiles all round, a water heater sets, towels and other things. It was indeed splendid. In the kitchen, Princess saw things she had never seen before. She looked like a villager who came to the city for the first time.

"Anny, what do we use this for?" Princess asked touching the blender.

"It's for blending things like tomatoes, pepper, onions and other things needed for cooking."

Princess was thrilled by Anita's humble abode.

"At last I have gotten a place to stay and have a quiet life, free from any encumbrance without anyone knowing my whereabouts." Princess said to herself.

Anita prepared food for the two of them in a jiffy. They ate, drank, gist, laughed and cracked jokes.

"Are you married?" Princess asked, switching the topic.

"What marriage?"

"Yes, I mean marriage."

"No, no, no forget that for now."

"Aren't you a woman? You think you will remain unmarried throughout your life?"

"Is there anything special about a man? What is it that he can do that I can't do better?" Anita asked proudly.

"But God has made him the head and I feel he should always be the head and . . ." Princess said.

"Oh you mean the woman should be the tail—a dumping ground for the man, right?"

"The woman is a helper; therefore both man and woman are companions but the man is the head".

"Alright, Pastor, let's put that topic in abeyance please," Anita said laughing.

"Alright, if you say so," Princess conceded.

Princess noticed Anita's closeness. She would always want to either touch Princess or hold her. Princess thought it was the normal closeness a crony would show. That first night however, Princess noticed some things somehow funny but she overlooked them.

Anita left for work the following day. Being left alone in the house, Princess took her time to see the rooms properly. She had a glance into Anita's album and not even a single picture of a man was there. "Does it mean that Anita has no boyfriend? Could that be the reason why she refused to discuss marriage the previous day?" Princess wondered.

As she was tidying up the room that morning, she saw an envelope addressed to Anita. She became curious, so she opened it and in it was a love letter written to Anita by a girl named Stella. 'Stella is a female name. Could Stella be a name for both male and female? If no, how could a female have written a love letter to another female? Could she be a lesbian?' Princess continued to wonder. It was possible because Anita has no business with men. "But if she is, what shall I do?" Princess soliloquized. Princess stood between the devil and the deep blue sea. She later made up her mind for anything as far as she would remain happy and her whereabout is not known to the world.

That evening after work, Anny bought lots of assorted gifts for Princess. She was enraptured and she expressed her joy openly. Anny grabbed her and gave a buss. She did not say a word though that looked strange.

Anita was an experienced lesbian who was wooed by one of her teachers in her semi-final year in the High School. Since then she had no business or relationship with a man. She has gone so deep into lesbianism that she could not stay alone. A fellow lesbian must be with her. She hated men with rabid hatred and out-rightly disgraced all men that approached her for relationship.

Being an old and experienced hand, Anita always played the role of a man. Her duty was to woo and court a girl. Just as a randy frolicked with other girls, so was Anny. She wooed by all means any beautiful girl with captivating features. That was why she could not take her eyes off Princess the first time they met in the police custody.

All through Anny's life, she had had affairs with many other lesbians. The last was a damsel with whom she fought over some money, which led to her detention. That was when she met Princess in police custody.

After supper, the cat was let out of the bag in a tactical and systematic manner. She brought out her photo album and a bunch of letters.

"Nana take this," Anita said as she give the letters to Princess. "Read all of them." So Princess took the letters and after reading them, Anita gave her about twelve pictures of the same person.

"What are all these for?" Princess asked.

"What did you observe?" Anny replied.

"Letters by Stella as well as her pictures."

"You are right! Now wait and see." She packed all the letters and pictures in a basin. She called Princess and they went out. She dropped everything on the ground and set fire on them, burned them to ashes.

"Why are you burning them?" Princess asked.

"She is out of my life.' Anny answered

"How?"

"You will understand."

Back into the room, Anita looked at Princess closely.

'Do you know that you are very beautiful?' Anny said.

Princess hung her head in shame.

"I want you to be very close to me always. I will always be there for you. You see, I love you so much and I will do anything to make you happy." As Anita said these words, she began to caress Princess.

Gradually they became agog with curiosity.

That day marked the beginning of her journey in the world of lesbianism. Each day before leaving home, Anny would give Princess books and videotapes on lesbianism. Princess read and watched a lot about lesbianism. Anny brainwashed Princess with heresies saying that God allowed man to live a free life so anyone can choose to live the way they wanted. "All that matters is the way you serve your God and that's all." Anny said. Princess was fully convinced by Anny's 'God Theory of Lesbianism'.

Within a short time, she became so deeply involved that at times she was surprised at herself. She learned and assimilated everything about lesbianism.

One day a girl knocked on the door.

"Who are you looking for:" Princess asked as she opened the door.

"Anny," replied the girl.

'She's not in."

"And who are you?' the stranger asked.

"What business do we have together?" Princess questioned her.

"Let me in!" the girl commanded.

"No!" Princess said, blocking the entrance.

Knowing well that the girl was the person Anny burnt her pictures and letters, Princess refused to let her in. Perhaps she has come to ask Anny for forgiveness. Despite all efforts to get in, the girl could not as Princess banged the door and went in.

"You foolish harlot, I will be back to teach you a lesson you'll never forget. Just wait for me," the girl said as she walked away.

When any came back, Princess told her all that happened between the lady and herself to Anny. Anny comforted her and told her that she would take care of the situation.

'You shouldn't allow that idiot into this room. She is very contumacious, disingenuous, dullard and recalcitrant. Let her know I don't want to set my eyes on her any longer. Don't associate with her in any way because that girl is dangerous.'

Normally, a lesbian gets jealous anytime she catches or hears that her prey is being wooed, enticed or harboured by another lesbian. Anny was afraid of Stella because she could woo Princess and go with her. That was why she tried everything to set them apart.

Later that evening somebody knocked on the door.

"What do you want again?" Princess asked as she opened the door.

"Is Anny in?"

"Anita," Princess called. "It's that girl."

"Let her in" Anita instructed.

"What do you want in my house Stella?" Anny asked.

"Who is that girl, Anny?" Stella asked.

"How is that your business?" Anny responded

". . . and what is she doing here?"

"Look Stella, enough of your trouble. You brought policemen and arrested me the last time after a simple misunderstanding over money, and today you are here again. Well, even if you want to apologize, I don't need your apology any longer. You can hold it to yourself . . ."

"You idiot . . ." Stella interrupted ". . . how dare you . . ."

35

"What! You have the gut to call me an idiot in my own house?"

Anny stood up and moved closer to her.

"Alright, get out" Anny said pointing to the door.

'Get out or I call the police.' Stella kept mute. Anny became furious and gave her a slap.

"You slapped me?"

Angered by the slap, Stella retaliated and both girls started fighting.

Princess joined in the fight on Anita's side without invitation. She held Stella's right leg and pulled it strongly and she fell on the floor and they gave her the beating of her life. They tore her clothes in pieces, leaving her with wounds all over her body and blood running through her nostrils. Anny only had a little cut around her neck.

Neighbours who came could not gain entrance until the whole show was over. Anita finally opened the door and pushed Stella out. A woman, who saw and had compassion on Stella, gave her a wrapper to cover herself up. Later, Stella invited a policeman and arrested Princess and Anita. They spent the night in police custody. They were released the following day after coming to compromise on the issue.

Princess was restless throughout the event. She brooded:

"Why am I always wanted by the police wherever I go? Who knows if the police at Koke have already signaled those at this station, I will be caught and that will be another big trouble for me. Now that I've been known by the police though with a fake name, my facial appearance might be an easy way of getting me. Something has to be done and immediately too; but how? Should I tell Anita the truth about myself? Would she be able to help me out? What if I have a problem with her just like Stella, won't she reveal the secret? But she looks good and I don't think there will be any problem. After all, we have promised to be together forever. I just have to tell her everything. Probably she might use her ingenuity to help me out. Moreover, I have to contribute to the feeding and buying of other things needed in the home. I can't be a dependent all through my life. I cannot be staying indoors all through my life. But how can I go out without anyone noticing me if I don't tell Anita the truth? If she gets to discover herself, she wouldn't be happy and that will be another trouble for me. Oh my God! What will I do?"

So one evening, after Anita returned from work, the two went out for shopping. They were to go to a nearby supermarket. After shopping, they were about crossing the road when Princess saw a man she knew. He was her father's closest friend. Princess stopped suddenly in the middle of the road and without considering oncoming vehicles, she turned back and ran towards the opposite direction. A driver moving his car at high speed wanted to dodge her but lost control and ran into a stationary water tanker. People rushed to the scene of the accident to rescue the victims, but Princess refused to stay. Perhaps her father's friend might come back and see her. Anita wanted to wait at the scene for a while but on Princess' insistence they left.

Princess became nervous. She refused to eat and her countenance changed that night. Anita held her closely and made her lie down on her laps.

"What's the problem my dear?" Anita asked.

Princess remained mute.

"Look at me Nana. Please tell me what the problem is. Don't you confide in me again? I promise to do my best to help you if you can just trust me . . ."

"Anny," Princess called after a long silence. "I have a confession to make. This has been disturbing me for a long time but I had not been valiant enough to tell you, though I have it in mind to tell you at the right time. May be this is the right time. Everything I told you about myself was spurious. I have never told anyone about it. It was a secret but because of my confidence and trust in you. I feel I shouldn't hide it from you anymore. My real name is Princess and not Nana as I told you. I have parents, brothers, sisters . . . ," Princess narrated the whole annals of her life from birth to the date of the narration. Anita stared at her without a single word.

"Nana," Anita called in a soft tone. 'I'm sorry for all you passed through in life. It could happen to anyone else. No matter who a person is, he must have a past; so don't let your past be a reason for demoralization or discouragement. Look at the future and forget about the past. Your new slogan should be forward ever, backward never and . . ."

"Anny, the police might be after me for all the crimes I have committed," Princess interrupted.

"Look, my dear; there is no problem without a solution. We shall find a way out of your problem. Now cheer up and be happy. Can I now call you with your real name, Princess?"

"Why not? You can also call my second name, Belinda. 'But . . .'"

"What?" Anita cut-in.

"I prefer Princess."

"That's alright king's daughter," Anita concluded laughing.

Both girls went to bed thinking of possibilities of making Princess live happily without the police or anyone else discovering.

CHAPTER FOUR

THE IMPERSONATION

"Would that be possible?" Princess asked.

"Why not," Anita replied. Nothing is impossible on earth except we decide to make it so."

What if people get to know about it?" interrupted Princess.

"Know about it? How? Is there any feature and characteristic common to man and woman? If there are, then a man is a different being whereas a woman is absolutely another being altogether. Or do you think that it's possible for a man to change into a woman or a woman into a man?

"No" Princess noted.

". . . then what is your fear? Relax and see what I, Anita, the wisdom lady will do."

'Almighty miss Wisdom, go ahead and make the impossible possible.' Princess added with laughter.

The girls alighted from the cab at the city terminus and headed towards the ultra-modern market. From afar, one could see the beautiful blue and white paint of the market radiating—people moving up and down from one hall to another transacting various businesses. The overt market opened daily from six o'clock in the morning and close at six in the evening. It was such a large place that strangers could easily get missing especially when they are not careful. At times, a person could be moving towards an entrance thinking it is an exit but before he realizes, he would be in another section of the market. In the crowd are thieves in their large number, going about. A person dared not handle their money or belonging carelessly else it will disappear in a jiffy. Diaries and organizers kept in pockets were often stolen under the mistaken belief that they are wallets probably containing money.

Princess followed Anita closely into the market like a lamb being led to the slaughter slab. They went to a boutique where men's wears are sold, especially jeans trousers and the lesbians bought many different coloured jeans. Some rough jeans commonly referred to as 'Rasta jeans' were sold there as well, and they bought some. Those were the kind of jeans trousers worn by rough guys when they go to parties or clubs in that city.

They bought shirts, face caps of various shapes, sizes and colours as well as different eyeglasses, but giving priority to dark ones. Also not left out in the purchase spree were different pairs of men's shoes including canvas, sneakers and boots. The lesbians also bought different types of wares.

In another hall in the market, Princess and Anita bought clipper and men's kind of belt. The other things they bought include a bag of cement, slim tea, lime, men's wristwatch and stockings. At another super market, they bought a set of bra-top and different sets of girdle.

The shopping came to an end when Anita's money got finished. "At least we've gotten the most important things we needed." said Anita. We will get the few left some other day.' Princess nodded in affirmation. So the lesbians boarded a taxi home and rested after eating the snacks they bought at a patisserie.

"Now it's time for you to test your new outfit," Anita began afterwards. Princess quickly jumped out of bed while Anita was busy removing the things bought from the bag. Princess picked a jean trouser and wore it.

"How do I look?" asked Princess.

"Wonderful! But put on the shirt first." Anita answered.

When Princess was about putting on the shirt, Anita drew her attention to the girdle and the bra-top'.

"Oh I have forgotten, please get them for me." She was given the girdle and bra-top and she wore both. The girdle is an undergarment for women, meant to hold the flesh firm whereas the bra-top is a woman's close fitting under garment worn to support, tighten and hold the breasts firm. After wearing the girdle and bra-top, she put on a fine blue shirt.

"Tuck in please," Anita said.

Princess glanced at her.

"I'm serious," said Anita laughing.

She picked a canvas and put it on after putting on the stockings.

"What else?" Princess asked.

Put on the fly-over and remove your earring.

"But men wear earring," Princess said.

"Yes, but not this type; men's earring is small with tiny pin."

"Oh yes, I think I have that type." Princess said.

Anita opened the wardrobe and brought a tiny pin earring.

'Just put on one on your left ear,' Anita told Princess. Princess put on the earring on her left ear and immediately ran to the mirror stand to see how she appeared.

"I told you earlier that you are now a MR. Do you still doubt me? Now you've seen yourself. Tell me now who you are?" Princess did not say a word. In her silence she starred at Anita, touching her long, admirable, dark, shinning hair.

"There is one more thing to make you complete." Anita said

"What's that?" Princess asked.

"Your hair?" Anita answered.

"My hair? You mean I should have it cut?"

"What do you think?" Anita asked.

"But there are men with long air and . . ."

"Oh! You want people to look at you with askance?" Anita interrupted.

"But, Anny my . . ."

"What's all this Princess? why the caprice? We have since discussed about this and you want to change your mind?'

"Alright, sorry please. Let's go ahead," Princess consented.

Anita brought out the clipper.

". . . but I haven't used this before. Should we call someone to help us?"

"Why?" Princess asked. "You want someone to know our secret? Maybe that would be at subsequent times but not this initial stage. The secret must be kept between one heart in two bodies," she concluded.

"Alright, let me give it a trial." She read all the instructions on the operating manual of the clipper. She connected it to electricity and asked Princess to sit down. She spread a wrapper around Princess' shoulder so that the hair would not drop on her body. Anita deepened the clipper into princess' hair and it crept beyond the expected level. She became disappointed in herself.

"I have made a mistake Princess." Anita said.

"What is it?"

"I crept beyond the limit I wanted to cut."

"Alright, just shave everything."

Anita cut the whole of Princess' hair without a single hair left on her head. Being a hairy person, Princess had little hair on her chin. Anita did not cut it to convince all 'doubting Thomases' that Princess is a man.

Princess went to the mirror stand and looked at herself with dark glasses on.

"This can't be me!" she exclaimed.

"Are you a villager? How can you not know yourself?" Anita said laughing. Princess looked round again and again.

"At last, this is a perfect man!" Anita exclaimed, "What do we call you now?

What do you mean? You are now a man and so people must know you with a male name."

"That's alright."

"So what do we call you?"

"I don't know," Princess replied.

"Well. I will give you a name and that will be eh—eh Boniface."

"No, no no! I don't like Boniface."

"Alright, I will give you a name in the Bible."

"That's better. So what name?"

"You want to know?"

"Yes."

"You really want to know?"

"Yes," replied Princess, waiting.

"You will be called Judas." Anita said laughing.

"What? Judas? What sort of name is that? Oh, Anny I don't like it. Why will you call me Judas? Am I a betrayer?" Princess said changing her countenance.

"Okay, we'll call you James."

"James is a good name. He was one of the twelve disciples of Jesus Christ"

"Mr. James come please." Anita called

As Princess walked towards her, she stopped her and she said:

"Is that how men walk?" come on, walk like James let me see." Princess walked over to Anita and she gave her a clap as she imitated men's step.

Princess had initially agreed on a possible way of disguising herself to enable her live freely. The lesbians felt that if Princess now changed her identity to that of a man, no one would ever identify or recognize her. Not even any of her family members, her old friends Queen and Benny or the police. Since Princess was new to the environment, it was possible for people to accept her new identity because naturally there are men with women features and vice versa. The lesbians have also planned that Princess would pretend to be partially dumb. She can hear but cannot speak and would rather use her hands to communicate.

To build up her physical structure and probably develop muscles, Princess began to do regular exercises. She would wake up in the morning, run a little distance, do press up and weight lifting. She produced weight lifting equipment using car wheels, cement and various objects of different sizes and weights. Princess had learned this from her elder brother when she was still at home. Gradually she began to build up, her chest expanded and her shape changed. With the frequent use of the girdle and bra top, she became like a man.

Anita's neighbours began to gossip. They called her all sorts of names. Some called her a harlot and others a prostitute because they thought she lived with a man. Princess became a gigolo in disguise.

One evening when Anita returned from work, she came into the room laughing.

"What is funny?" Princess asked.

"It's our neighbours" she answered.

"What happened?" Princess asked.

"I was just told that they are calling me all sorts of names. Some say I live with a fellow lady but now I'm staying with a gigolo."

"Wow! That's good news!" Princess exclaimed.

"Thank God that people have really believed that I'm a man. That means I have really changed my identity. I can now move out confidently."

Princess began to jump and run round the room.

Princess became so built and man structured. All her female clothes became Anita's. Men's wears became her permanent clothes. At home, she became a man-woman while outside she was a woman-man.

Strangers rarely come to Anita's house but whenever someone called, Princess was always addressed as "sir". That gave her more courage and confidence to carry on her behaviour.

To advance her plans, Princess joined a karate club at a nearby gymnasium. That marked the genesis of Princess' interaction with men. In the morning she would do her exercise at home while in the evening she went for karate training at the gymnasium. To further disguise herself, Princess began to smoke cigarettes. Anita always gave her money for the cigarettes. Princess was always seen with packet of cigarettes but she did not smoke at home or when she was alone. Normally when many people gather she would bring out her cigarettes and smoke. She introduced herself at the gymnasium as James. She became very popular because of her jovial nature and was fond of making people laugh always. She had the advantage of learning fast because of her determination.

Every evening after work, Anita would go to the gymnasium to watch Princess train. She would relax there at times sipping her favourite pineapple juice and snacks. At the end of the training, the lesbians would go home together. So, Princess introduced Anita to her friends as 'his' fiancée. Not knowing they are lesbians, people so much admired them as some said they would make a very good and happy family.

No one ever suspected Princess to be a woman except that people said she had feminine voice. That wasn't anything at all because there was also a boy at the gymnasium who had a woman structure and did things like a woman. Princess at times mocked him by calling him Madam Joe. He would get angry sometimes and insult Princess.

One day, Anita took Princess to her place of work and introduced her as her fiancé. Everyone there liked the impersonated James because he looked cool, handsome, quiet, jovial and well built. Whenever Anita told Princess about people's positive comment, Princess would jump up and run round the room and hug her. At times she would pick glasses and any available drink for a toast to that. When no drink was available in the house, Princess would get glasses of water and go to Anita for a toast.

However, all that occupied Princess' mind was her permanent freedom.

"Do you think someone will someday recognize me?" Princess asked one morning.

"Why such a question?" Anita asked.

"Is there any problem?"

"'No . . . but I feel . . .'"

"Feel what?" Interrupted Anita . . . that you will be caught?' With this kind of wisdom we have exhibited, no man, not even one either born of a woman directly or indirectly can suspect that you are a woman. Not even the devil can! What more of mortal man?'

One beautiful Sunday evening, someone knocked on the door while the lesbians were in the room. They never minded who it is that is at the door. As the knock persisted, Princess dressed properly, walked to the door and opened it.

"Good evening sir," the man greeted.

"Yes what do you want?" Princess asked

"I want to see Anita." The man answered.

"And who are you?" Princess asked hurriedly.

"Benson is my name."

She banged the door behind her and went in.

Within a short while Anita came out with Princess.

"Benson, what?" Inquired Anita.

"I just came to . . ."

"To do what? (Anita cut in) Haven't I warned you not to come near me again? By the way, who gave you my house address?" He stood speechless.

"Now leave my house immediately," Anita commanded.

"Look Anita, let me just have a word with you," Benson pleaded.

Anita spoke with Princess and they allowed him come inside. He began his long story from when he first saw Anita, how he felt for her and how he so much loved her but Anita didn't even greet him talk more of reciprocating his love.

"Is that all?" Anita asked.

"Yes, but all I want from you is to give me a chance to prove myself"

"Alright, get out!"

Benson kept quiet.

"I said get out!" she shouted

Princess quickly ran out of the inner room on hearing Anita's voice.

"What's the matter dear?" Princess asked playing the part of a man.

"It's this shameless man coming in here to tell me that he loves me."

Angered by the man's words, Princess went straight to him.

"Leave this house!" she commanded pointing to the door.

"How will I leave?" asked Benson.

"Are you challenging him?" Anita shouted.

"Is it your house?" Benson asked Princess.

"What do you mean?"

"Are you Anita's husband?" What is then your business with me? I'm here for the same purpose for which you came also. So, I advise you to let sleeping dogs lie.

Princess became furious and from nowhere she turned back and gave Benson a heavy blow on the neck with her feet. Benson fell on the chair. She watched him recover. After Benson had fully recovered, she moved to the door, opened it and directed Benson to move out. Without a word, he walked out of the house silently.

Anita was so happy at the incidence. She was now sure of protection from her lesbian lover. She held Princess by the hand and led her to the room. Anita put her head on Princess' laps as she looked up on her face.

'I want to learn about this karate,' Anita said.

'Wow!' Princess exclaimed. 'I will teach you if you are ready and serious. I will give you a general background of what karate is all about and a little lecture after which we'll go into the practical which is the most important'.

"If you teach me, I will in no time know more than you," Anita said, smiling.

I love it that way. 'But you should know that you couldn't learn karate on a platter of gold. You have a price to pay. You must sacrifice both human and material resources and above all determination and endurance must be your watchwords'. Princess told her.

"Karate is a form of unarmed combat in which a person or someone kicks or strikes with the hand, knees, feet and even elbow. You understand right?"

"Yes," Anita nodded.

"It is one of the various forms of unarmed combat known as martial arts. It is a very dangerous game because a blow can cripple or even kill, and normally blows are aimed at delicate parts of the body like the stomach and neck."

"Oh! Is that why you hit Benson in the neck?" Anita asked. Both laughed.

"Don't mind the idiot," Princess replied as she continued. "There are different forms of karate. We have the Chinese karate, Okinawa, Japanese and the Korean. The Chinese karate is called 'Kung fu', while the Korean is known as 'tae kwon do'. The latter lay more emphasis on kicking while the former uses a flowing, circular motion that differs from the movement of others. Anny, you should also know that all these types of karate are of the same techniques but each of them stresses specific skills and has its own style of movement."

"But why do people use the same uniform with different belts?" Anita asked.

"Normally both students and teachers alike wear pyjamas-like costume and a different colour of belt. The belt signifies the rank of a trainer. Beginners wear the white belt while experts wear black. For those who are in their intermediary level like me, use brown, green or purple depending on the rank." Princess explained.

"Why does a person yell when throwing blows?"

"Yes, in trying to kick, punch or strike, there is a need to yell. Sound is very important. When a person yells, say 'yah,' he puts maximum force into the blow. Apart from that, he can also yell before striking in order to startle his opponent."

"Thanks for that wonderful lecture."

"You are welcome but I have to give you a test."

"Test?"

"Yes of course."

"No, I can't."

"Why?"

"It is as if you spoke in a strange language. All you said got in through the right ear and it is gone out through the left."

"Wow-oh! You mean I have just wasted my time talking. Well, if all I have said entered through the right ear and went out through the left, then there is nothing in the brain to hold it," said Princess.

"Hey Princess, you think I'm that dull?" At least I can tell you what you've just said but I can't remember all those terminologies.

"Anyway the theory is not so important. So when do we start the practical? Princess asked.

Anita kept quiet and Princess gave her a slight blow on the shoulder in the name of practical. Anita shouted.

"I don't want the practical again? I don't even need the karate anymore!"

The lesbians continued their gist and played until they slept off.

CHAPTER FIVE

THE ASYMMETRICAL GUY

Nothing seemed to be as interesting as being together for the lesbians. They felt as if the whole pleasure in the world ends in their humble abode. Nothing was ever an impediment to their affair. Every morning, while Anita prepared for work, Princess got busy with her regular exercises. Princess would see Anita off for work every blessed day. She prepared lunch in the afternoon while in the evening she went to the gymnasium for karate training. After work, Anita would join Princess and they would go back home together.

Princess continued her karate training to the advance stage. At this stage she was often appointed to teach beginners. But she still claimed to be half deaf. She pretended to be unable to actually communicate as expected. This notwithstanding, her special way of communication attracted secret admirers. She was always given the opportunity to train. Communication barrier made Princess lost a lucrative job when a karate club was looking for a teacher. A team of judges at a karate competition recommended her for the job but after due consultation, it was discovered that the impersonated 'he' could not effectively communicate. She lost it to someone else.

Princess became so free that she began to go to nightclubs and attend parties with her darling Anita. They went to the market and other public places together and also attended public functions any time they were invited.

The lesbians avoided making close friends and their sheer closeness made people who intend to come closer to stay away, because one would feel they were husband and wife.

After sometime, Princess felt there was no point staying at home since she was already undoubtedly a man. To her, if she begins to work, that would reduce the burden on Anita who had never complained. When Princess told Anita about her plan to start work she became angry and out-rightly opposed that decision. Anita had a mixed feeling about Princess' idea of work because she thought if Princess start working, she would have enough for herself and that means she would be intending to have her independence. She might probably get money, pick another lesbian and forget about Anita. Anita was full of suspicion because a similar incident occurred some years back when a lesbian lover abandoned her after making money. After moments of arguments and promises, Anita agreed that they should search for a job. For the fact that Princess had no qualification to deserve a white-collar job, she was ready for any type of job as long as it could fetch her money.

After closing from work, Anita would go round town looking for at least a suitable job for Princess. She intimated her colleagues to help whenever there was any vacancy.

One day, before the morning session at work, a colleague came to Anita and told her that someone bought a truck and was looking for a truck assistant.

"What sort of nonsense is this?" Anita shouted.

"Nonsense? How?"

"James as a truck assistant? God forbid!"

"I thought you said any type of job will be alright for your fiancé."

"But of all jobs on earth, is that the only one you could get?"

"Well I'm sorry," the woman answered.

Anita's rejection of the job was due to numerous reasons. She thought if Princess began to work as truck assistant, she would be detected easily. Apart from that, she would not have time to spend with her again. It also means that a lacuna would be created in the relationship. When Princess heard about the new job, she gave an outright rejection of it.

"Taking this job is tantamount to trading on slippery ground," she said. The lesbians who were not ready to miss themselves made up their minds that they would only work within that town and nowhere else.

While returning from work one warm evening, Anita saw a vacancy signpost indicating that a hotel was looking for a barman.

"This might be a manageable place for Princess," Anita thought. She went into the hotel premises and asked of the manager. He was not on seat.

Anita met a gentle lady who was introduced as the deputy manager.

"Good evening madam," Anita greeted genuflecting.

"Hello my dear, you are welcome. How can I help you?"

I have someone who would like to work in your hotel. He is a young and strong guy, very active and zealous and endures hard labour. But the only problem is that he cannot communicate properly and . . .'

"Hey girl' interrupted the woman "How do you expect a dumb to work in a hotel? How would he serve in a hotel? How would he carry out his responsibilities?"

"It's not that he cannot hear completely madam, he can understand what a person says; only that the response is always difficult. At times he utters some words out but cannot speak fluently."

"Alright, let him come and see me tomorrow so that I can assess him."

"Thank you madam." Anita answered and left.

Anita left the hotel and headed for the gymnasium where Princess was to engage a man who challenged her in a combat. She had told Anita the previous day that she was afraid of that man because he was an expert and his strength and duration of endurance was more than hers. But because Princess had made a lot of noise telling everyone that she could face him, she wouldn't like her colleagues at the gymnasium and her opponent to call her names. Princess had made up her mind to do her best. Anita encouraged her to try hard so that she could defeat the giant.

Anita arrived when they were about to commence. It was a free fighting contest, so it was going to be without any pre-arranged technique. And as one of the rules, a contestant score mark when he delivers a blow that majority of judges consider effective. Princess seemed not to be afraid because her teacher had given her simple techniques of dealing with her opponent.

At the venue of the contest, spectators sat round the big hall and there were four judges and one referee. Princess' supporters began to shout her name 'James! James!! James!!!' They clapped to rhyme with the chanting of her name. On the other side, the supporters were playing drums and singing the name 'Jackson'. Both Jackson and James began to exhibit various skills at the beginning of the contest. Princess gave the first blow of the fight when she surprised Jackson using a technique her master taught her. The crowd went wild with excitement.

Half way into the fight, Princess had almost equaled points with Jackson as she applied more sophisticated techniques but the physical ability and endurance of the man superseded hers.

Towards the end of the fight, Princess became fatigued and retarded in her blows. Jackson took advantage of that and gave her effective blows and he won the fight.

Jackson was presented the winning medal while Princess got the runner-up medal.

As soon as the lesbians got into their room, they began to laugh.

"You amazed me," Anita said. 'How did you manage to fight that man so well?'

"I really gave out my whole best. Thank God that some of the techniques I used were not known to him. Otherwise, I would have run out of that place . . . ."

"You fought a man and almost won!!! What would have happened if it were a fellow woman?"

"But he gave me correct blows,"

"Oh sorry, it's over," Anita said unable to control her laughter.

Anita helped Princess to pull off her costumes. She warmed water, which Princess used for her bath, after which Anita massaged Princess' body and applied balm all over her body. She also took some pain-relieving drugs and afterward they ate and rested for the night.

Princess remained indoors throughout the following day after Anita left for work. Because of the pain of the fight the previous day, all she did for the day was, eat, took her pain relieving tablets, had her bath and slept off.

That evening, when Anita returned, Princess was watching a movie while lying down on the rug. As soon as she opened the door, Anita shouted "James! James!! James!!!" clapping her hands as demonstrated the previous day at the gymnasium. Princess could not help but laughed and laughed until the room became noisy as if a laughter gas has just exploded there. So it was, anytime Anita wanted to laugh, she would start clapping, chanting "James! James!! James!!!"

Afterward, the lesbians went to the hotel to see the woman as scheduled. The hotel was not as big as the one Princess went to the first day she came to town. It was a big building situated beside an artificial water dam. The reception was at the entrance to the right where the bar and the banquet hall were situated. On the opposite direction was a restaurant while adjacent to the bar was a room for lodging. There was an open space in the middle of the hotel with a mighty tree at the centre. Around it were canopies arranged in an attractive decoration. Flowers surrounded the whole environment.

When they got to the office of the madam, the lesbians sat down.

"You are welcome," the madam said. "Are you the man that wants to work here?"

Princess nodded in affirmation.

"What is your name?"

"Please give him a paper and pen," Anita interrupted.

Princess tried to explain any question asked by gestures but anyone the madam did not understand, Princess would write it down.

When the woman discovered that Princess knew karate and was physically built, coupled with the fact that 'he' could fairly communicate, she decided to give 'him' a trial.

Princess began work the following week. She performed her duties with all seriousness and diligence. Every morning, the lesbians would go to work together as husband and wife. They parted ways at a junction while after work Anita would go to the hotel and wait for Princess till she has closed.

At the hotel, Anita was known as James's fiancé. She would sit while Princess went about her normal duty. Sometimes when there are many customers, Anita would help in serving under Princess' Instruction.

At the end of each month, the girls would put their salaries together, buy all necessary things and save the remainder.

After about a year and some months, Princess had become a popular figure at the hotel. James became the common name called by regular customers. For the fact that the impersonated lesbian was gentle, decorous and affable, many liked her and gave her money in return for her good services. Princess enjoyed her work in the dual identity as James the bar man in the hotel while she continued in her lesbianism.

One evening, Anita went to the hotel to wait for her lesbian lover as usual. Three men sitting at the open space near the door called her—though she did not know who they were and why they called, she went to them. They told her to sit down but she refused.

"Please young girl, join us and enjoy yourself," one of the men said.

"Oh yes! Girls like you deserve better treatment," one of the men added. Anita turned about to go when one of the men reached out his hand and held her by the wrist. He drew her closer to him.

"A beautiful girl like you should not waste her time with a common bar man who is even almost dumb."

"Leave my hand," Anita spoke angrily. He insisted and demanded that Anita wait and listen to what he had to say. Princess noticed the scene from afar and watched with keen interest as Anita struggled to disengage the man's hand. Just in a jiffy, Princess appeared, jumped up and scattered the whole table with her foot. She kicked the table which went down with two of the men sitting by it. Beer poured on their bodies and one had a cut from a broken bottle. The man who escaped falling down picked a bottle of beer and wanted to break it on Princess' head, but before he did that, Princess rolled and seized his legs and he fell to the ground on his head and blood began to gush out. People rushed to the scene. Some held Princess by the hands while others held the man.

There arose a sudden hubbub as every party tried to explain their own side of the story. Anita did the talking while Princess just looked at people angrily. When one of the men attempted to call the police, the manager who just entered stopped him and invited them to his office where Anita and the men presented their cases. The manager used his dexterity in handling the problem. He warned Princess not to fight customers again and he apologized to the customer promising that nothing like that would repeat itself. The manager offered to take the injured men to the hospital for treatment but they refused.

As soon as the men left the manager's office, they left the hotel premises. When the men left, the manager called Princess and Anita and apologized for what happened. He told them that whenever some people see a girl in a hotel, they felt she was the promiscuous type, so they would attempt to do all sorts of nonsense. Apart from that, the men were drunk at the time of the incident. So, the two girls left the manager's office and Princess went back to her work.

Princess continued her pretenses and living with dual identity in spite of all the happenings. Never for once had someone suspected her. She was constantly with one ear-ring on her left ear and always in different men's wears, with jackets at all times and low hair cut. She associated mostly with a boy that worked in the hotel. The only business Princess had with her female colleagues was just greeting or carrying out joint duty when it is necessary.

While working at the hotel, Princess had another encounter that almost exposed her secret. One morning, while preparing to go to work, the lesbians heard a knock on the door. On opening, they saw two policemen and the hotel manager.

"What happened?" Princess asked hurriedly.

"You are Mr. James right?" one of the policemen asked.

"Yes, any problem?" Princess asked.

"You are wanted at the police station to give an explanation."

"About what?"

"Robbery in the hotel."

"When? How?"

Princess began to shiver. She thought her secret had been exposed and the police had probably traced her. Could it be that they have traced her in connection with the fight at the party leading to someone's death or the death of the albino in the hotel or the impersonation itself?

Princess got a relief when she saw that the five boys that worked in the hotel were all there at the station. They were told that robbers broke into the hotel and went away with the money made from sales within the week, which was intended to be taken to the bank the following day. The robbers also made away with other valuables, which when the police interrogated the guard, he said that the gang consisted of five boys, mentioning the names of the gang members; he also described their roles and how the robbery took place.

All the boys, including Princess were surprised at the fabrication but there was nothing they could do than to wait for God's intervention. After writing their statements, their bodies were searched. They were asked to remove all they had in their pockets. They also removed their shoes. Princess was asked to remove her pullover, which had been her constant wear since she assumed her second identity as a man. She refused but the policemen threatened and she complied. Now, without the pullover jacket and being closely associated with other guys in the cell, Princess felt her secret would reveal; so she changed her countenance and began to shed crocodile tears. Throughout their stay in the cell, Princess didn't look at any of her colleague's face. She stayed far away from them claiming that she was worried shocked by the fabricated story.

What made her fear most was the fact that if the police would interrogate them, there was the tendency of her secret being revealed because, her cloth would be removed which would lead to discovery of her true identity?

At night, the guard and the suspects were called. The police officer asked the guard to narrate all that happened the previous day

"Sir, (he began), these people didn't know anything about the robbery. I only mentioned their names so as to save myself from the hands of the policemen who tortured me. I just mention their names so that the investigation officer will stop torturing me." The officer became furious and left.

So it was, the following morning, two officers came back and asked the guard to repeat what he said the previous night. He repeated his words and they left and then Princess and the boys were later released on bail.

The experience in the cell was not pleasant at all. It was a small room with little holes that hardly allow air in for ventilation. As congested as the cell was, it also served as toilet. In nutshell, it was everything to its occupants. Because of the way it was built, one could hardly differentiate between night and day in there. Other non-human friends that kept the cell tenants company included bedbugs and mosquitoes, which also provided free musical interlude at night. Princess likened it to the cage at the shrine because both experiences are synonymous.

After their release, Anita decided that Princess would no longer work in the hotel. Despite apologies from the hotel management, Princess refused to accept the offer. She felt once beaten, twice shy. She felt that if she continued, probably she might get into another problem that could lead to her exposure. Princess and Anita began to look for another job but for three months they were not successful, because of Princess' inability to communicate effectively.

CHAPTER SIX

THE DELIVERANCE

The condition of the lesbians was not so critical because at least, they have enough for themselves. Nevertheless, they have other plans to do other things such as buying a car and building their own house, but since Princess stopped working, their plans seemed threatened. Her karate business was not fetching her much money, as the game was not so lucrative, not much priority was given to it as other games such as football. As a result, Princess had no option but to remain at home all through her period of joblessness.

"If this continues, we will not actualize our dreams," Anita said.

"What should we do?" Princess asked. Anita sat for a while without uttering a word.

Some months back, Anita's colleague had invited her to visit her church. Anita had always refused the offer out-rightly. She believed that a supreme being called God exist but she did not really come to know about the worship of such a being.

She came from a polygamous family where nobody cares about the other—and throughout her lifetime, from childhood to adulthood, she didn't know the way to church, mosque or shrine. Even if she knew, it was when she passed by and saw people going in or coming out. Her father was a chronic drunkard who did not care about anything. His business was his utmost priority, while drinking followed. As for the mother, she spent most of her time struggling to meet the need of her nine children. The situation was so because the husband gave no money to any of his wives. The policy was self-striving for survival.

In the high school when students were made to attend fellowship under compulsion, Anita kept on dodging. She would always run to the house of the mistress who introduced her to the world of lesbianism. There she would spend her time. Her mates reported the case to the school matron, but her lesbian mistress always defends her.

Lynda had again given Anita an invitation to attend a revival in her church coming up at the weekend. She has also told Anita to come along with James. Prior to this latter invitation, Lynda had told Anita that it is possible for Princess to speak clearly again if the man of God prays for her. Anita did not see any reason to be excited about that promise of Lynda, because, Princess' partial dumbness was just a calculated plan. But Anita thought there is an opportunity in that, so she called Princes:

"Princess," Anita called. "Let's use this opportunity to go to the church since they say it is possible for a person to be healed after prayer. You will be prayed for and you will start talking . . ." She suggested

"But Anny, is that possible . . . ?"

"Of course yes! That will be called miracle."

"All right, I think that is right because the moment I start talking, I will get a job and that will accelerate the actualization of our dreams."

At work the following day, Anita told Lynda that she and her fiancé would be coming for the weekend revival programme.

The impersonated James dressed in her men's attire ready for the Friday programme, scheduled for six o'clock in the evening. There was no Bible in the house so Princess being the 'man', held a big novel whereas Anita held her handbag.

The church was a mighty building with beautiful decorations. As one walked on the isle, pews were arranged on both sides. The pulpit was made of glass and decorated with flowers. The Minister was right there on the altar. By the left side was the choir stands while the church band was on the opposite side.

The eight hundred-sitter auditorium was filled to capacity that Friday evening. The programme started with prayer followed by praise and worship. Princess and Anita danced as they had never done before. Both the choir and music band sang melodiously.

As soon as the preacher mounted the pulpit, he made some prophetic utterances:

"There will be a benison tonight"

"Amen!" Responded the congregation.

"God will heal someone tonight. You are in for deliverance from the bondage of sin and of Satan; you will be delivered from all curses." The congregation shouted a loud "Amen." He continued his message on God's capability stressing the fact that nothing was impossible with God. He said that God could heal whatever kind of sickness including the medically incurable Acquired Immune Deficiency Syndrome (AIDS). He added that God is a healer, a deliverer, a provider, a protector and a merciful God.

After the preaching, the pastor said he would pray for two sets of people: those who would like to repent from the evil ways and those who would want healing. When it was time for healing prayer, Princess refused to go to the altar, despite all effort by Anita to make her step forward.

When they were back at home, Anita expressed her disappointed with what Princess did. Princess apologized and told Anita that she became nervous and scared so she had to wait and watch to see how the whole thing would go. Actually, Princess was convinced of the healing because a paralyzed man walked after the prayer. Princess thought she had gathered much experience so she promised to go out for the prayer the following day.

During the service that Saturday evening, Princess got up from her seat and walked to the front. She knelt down with her two hands put together and her head down. When the preacher asked what the problem was, she only pointed to the ears and demonstrated that she could not hear. Her ears were anointed with oil and she was prayed for while Anita watched with keen interest. Immediately after prayer, Princess began to speak publicly.

"What is your name?" the preacher asked.

"James," she answered.

"Can you now say God has healed me?"

"God has healed me," Princess said. The preacher shouted "Praise the Lord" and the congregation responded with "Hallelujah."

After the service, the ushers led Princess to the pastor's office.

"James," the Pastor called. "God has healed you and your healing is permanent. You must praise and continue to serve God all through your life."

"By the way where do you live?" The pastor asked

"At Hill Crescent."

"Where do you work?"

"I'm not working."

"Why? Who feeds clothes and gives you shelter?"

"My girlfriend?"

"Your girlfriend?"

"Yes."

"You mean, you stay with your girlfriend?"

"Yes sir."

"Are you married?"

"No."

"James, an unmarried child of God doesn't stay with a girlfriend. It is only when you are married. Do you get me?"

"Yes sir."

"What's your girlfriend's name?"

"Anita."

"Anita, the Pastor called. It is not right for an unmarried girl like you to stay with James". That's only when you are married, is that alright?"

"Yes sir." Anita replied.

"As for you James, see me in my office on Tuesday so that we'll see how we can help you."

"Thank you sir," said the lesbians simultaneously.

They went back home happy because their plan had succeeded. But the problem was that the Pastor have known that they are staying together. He was against such relationship and will want them to stay separately. The lesbians felt if the church would give Princess a good job and accommodation, that would be a good development because it would not stop them from furthering their plans.

The following Sunday, Princess went to church and gave her testimony to the amazement of all those who had known her before. To further protect herself, the impersonated James went to her former hotel and told them of the miraculous healing.

In the Pastor's office that Tuesday as planned, the pastor told Princess that the church had decided to provide a job for her at the Church office with an appreciable salary, and as for accommodation, a brother in the church who occupied a single room volunteered to accommodate her pending the time she would get her own apartments.

Anita was happy about the development but gave Princess strict warnings.

"Don't let our secrets out. The man you are going to stay with must know you as a man. Don't trust him for a minute. You must not be careless with your dressing. Remember to always be in your bra-top and girdle. Don't ever undress where someone is. Your dressing should be when the door is locked or in the bathroom. Also remember not to urinate anywhere outside. In a nutshell don't do anything that makes anyone, including that brother, suspect you're a woman . . ."

"Trust me Anny, I'm equal to the task . . ."

". . . But you will be coming to my place more frequent than I would to you, because our secret must be kept secret'! Both girls shouted in one accord.

Princess packed in on Saturday evening the following week.

"You are welcome," said the Church brother.

"Thank you."

They dropped her luggage and sat down.

"Well, Anny meet Tony, my good friend who offered to accommodate me and Tony, this is my fiancée."

Anita and Tony exchanged pleasantries.

The room was just a single room in a compound of about seven rooms. The well-cemented compound had a clean environment, a well-fortified wall and a gate. The room was carpeted with a single mattress, television and radio at one corner. There was also a hanger for clothes and a shoes bag. The tenants generally share the kitchen, bathroom and toilet since none of the rooms was self-contained.

Tony enjoyed staying with Princess very much because she made him laugh whenever they were together and she did a lot of funny things. At times she taught Tony karate. Tony did not even for once suspect he was living with a woman. All he said was that Princess had a female voice and she always countered by saying that it was God's doing.

Princess would go to work in the morning and return in the evening. At times, Anita would come and stay with her while at other times she would go to Anita's home. Tony was such a busy man who rarely stayed at home. He left very early and returned late. The only time they have to spend together was weekends.

Church activities became Princess' utmost priority. She attended all weekly activities. People began to call her brother James because of her commitment and dedication to church activities. But in her heart it was just a strategy to keep life moving. In fact that was the period that Princess advanced in her lesbian practice. The church only served as a proper cover-up for her fiddlesticks and obnoxious life.

She became a member of the music band of the church. Being a 'man' with a female voice' she sang so well and people loved her voice. Being a committed 'brother' in the church, she was often appointed to lead prayer meetings sometimes; she would speak in tongues as though heaven would come down. She was always with the prayer warriors.

One hot evening, when there was power outage, Tony and Princess lit a candle and lay down on the bed as they gist about the activities of the day.

"Bro James," Tony called. "Why is the weather so hot today?"

"I don't know"

"And you are still comfortable in your jacket with this heat?"

"Why not? I'm used to it." Princess responded.

Tony had noticed that Princess was always in jacket whether it was hot or cold. She never for once pulled off her clothes as men do. Tony was someone who would pull his clothes in the room anytime he was relaxing. Sometime he prefer sleeping with knickers but seeing his friend's body was like a taboo. That did not even raise any element of suspicion on Tony's mind.

"How about Anita?" Tony asked.

"She's fine"

"So when are you preparing to get married?"

"Married?" Princess asked laughing.

"Bro Tony, you must be funny . . . ?"

"Funny?"

"Yes, funny of course."

"Well, I feel you and your fiancée have come a long way and maybe sooner or later you people should call us to celebrate . . ."

"Yes," Princess interrupted. "We'll do that when I'm ready. At least, I need to get an apartment of my own, a car and other things before I think of a wife."

"James! James!! You think you can't marry until you get all you want on earth?"

"Bro Tony, my God is a great provider. He is capable and can provide all my needs according to his riches in glory . . ."

'Amen,' said Tony.

From Tony's discussion with Princess, no man could ever imagine, not even in a dream that Princess was an impersonated man. She told him concocted lies about her family background; how she grew up half dumb and her healing then she shared with Tony her future ambitions, hopes and aspirations.

CHAPTER SEVEN

THE REVELATION

There is a common adage: "The only difference between a lie and the truth is that truth stands the test of time whereas a lie only lasts for a short while". No matter how good, sweet, beautiful and perfectly arranged a lie may be, the good income will turn out to bad outcome, the sweet savour will turn out to be a decaying odour, and the ugly, beautifully dressed would be revealed.

That is why it is often said that nothing is hidden under the sun, no matter the length, breath or depth of that thing. The only thing that never disappoints is the truth. When you hold on to it, it will set you free and you will be free indeed. Indeed, freedom is living in truth as the good book has said.

Mrs. Sam, Anita's neighbour who knew Princess before her impersonation called Anita shortly after Princess' deliverance and said:

"Where is that your friend?"

"My friend, Princess?"

"Yes."

"She left long ago."

"But that your boyfriend, James looks like her—even her voice sounds like his."

"Eh, that is it; people can resemble each other . . ."

"But their resemblance is too much as if they have the same parents."

"Well that shows God's awesomeness," Anita said.

"Could this woman be suspicious?" Anita thought. She saw Princess when she first came but heard nothing about her later. She did not see James on arrival but noticed that Anita suddenly harbouring a guy. She has called Anita sometimes back to advise her on the danger of living with a man in her house without valid marriage. "This woman must have suspected something," Anita soliloquized. "But what is our business with her after all? Would she reveal the secret to the church? What proof has she when even a blind man can feel that Princess is a man? To hell with her!" Anita concluded.

Tony left for work at about seven o'clock one fateful Thursday. Unknown to him he picked the wrong key to his office cabinet. He had to return home to pick the key. As soon as he hurriedly opened the door, he saw Princess undressed. Princess did not expect anyone to come the moment Tony is gone—no one except Anita might call. So she forgot to shut the door as her usual practice was when preparing for work. As soon as Tony opened the door; she quickly picked a towel and covered herself. She was already in trousers trying to put on her bra-top and girdle when he came in.

"What happened?" she asked sitting on the mattress.

"I forgot my key."

"But you made me afraid . . ."

"How?"

"People don't come into the room as hurriedly as you did."

"Oh sorry James, I was really in haste."

Tony picked his key and left hurriedly. 'This is unusual. How could a man cover his body when he sees his fellow man?' Tony wondered. 'Could he be having skin disease that he doesn't want anyone to see? Tony thought that 'James' could be the type that liked privacy so much that they would not want to see their nakedness.

Princess became so disturbed that day. "Could it be that Tony has seen me in my nakedness?" Has he discovered that I'm not a man? But he seems not worried," Princess thought.

Immediately after work that day, Princess who had planned to attend the church Bible studies before going to Anita's place abandoned the church. She ran to Anita's house and explained all that happened. Anita comforted her by telling her that if Tony had seen her, he would have expressed some kind of shock but since he didn't, that means he did not really notice anything. But because of anything like that in future, Anita told Princess that they need to get a house so that Princess could stay on her own. So, they began to plan to get an apartment close to Anita's house.

The event that however, led to the revelation of Princess' secret was when she came in contact with an elderly man. Initially, the man saw her picture with a friend at the karate club.

"What is this person's name?" the man asked the Karate friend.

"James." The karate friend answered.

"Is this a man or woman?" The old man asked.

"What sort of question is that? He's a man of course; my karate friend."

"Where is he now?"

"He works in my church"

"Can you show me the place?" The man asked.

"Yes . . . but why are you so keen about this guy?"

"Don't worry, I'll explain," the man promised.

The following day, Frank brought the man to Princess' place of work. As soon as she saw him, she became nervous but pretended not to have an idea of whom he was.

"Princess" the man called. She turned her face to Frank's place discussing about events at the gymnasium.

"Can you hear me?" the man asked her again.

"Who are you talking to?" Princess asked.

"Are you not Belinda; a daughter of my friend Jones?"

"I don't understand what this man is talking about."

The man and Frank left after a while.

"I told you that he is James and you are calling him Princess. Is Princess a male name?"

"Look, you will not understand. She grew up in my hands. Even if she changes into a monster, I will recognize her." Frank kept on laughing as he went back home.

On Sunday, the man came to the church. Immediately after service, he went to the Pastor and intimated him that he would like to speak to him. He was asked to wait until the Pastor was through with a briefing with the elders after which he was invited in to see the pastor.

"Yes, good afternoon sir." The old man greeted

"How was the service?" The pastor asked

"Very fine sir."

"How may I help you?" the pastor asked.

"Yes, I'm Mr. Chike. I have something to discuss with you. As you can see, I'm an elderly man and I cannot come here to waste time on vain issues. I lived in Angelis town all through my life until my eldest son brought me to this city some few months ago for medical attention, because I have been ill. I saw something that seems so much a surprise to me, so I felt it's necessary to see you and talk it over." Chike cleared his throat and adjusted his sitting position "Some years ago, (he continued), my friend and neighbour Mr. Jones had a daughter whose name is Princess. I watched her growing up as a child until she got involved in some dangerous activities and committed serious offences in her High School days. Since then, she has been a fugitive. All efforts by the police to get her were to no avail. Some days back, I saw a picture of some men at a karate club in my son's house and I saw someone that looks exactly like Princess' but it was a man called James. I'm convinced that that man called 'James' is the Princess I know from childhood." "Pastor, the man continued, I want you to properly study this James. You may prove me wrong but I want a proper investigation to know his true identity."

"Thank you very much," said the pastor. But before Mr. Chike left, the Pastor asked all necessary information about Princess and her family and he collected Chike's contact address.

After evening service that day, the Pastor called Tony to his office.

"How are you Tony?" the pastor asked

"I'm fine Sir." Tony answered.

"And your colleague?"

"He's doing fine."

"Good," the Pastor answered.

"Are you really enjoying your stay with him?"

"Yes Sir, James is very nice and simple . . ."

"But how about his family, has he really been going home to see some of his relations?"

"Eh all he told me was that his parents are no more but I have not asked him about his relations."

"What of Anita?"

"She comes around at interval between three and four days to see him . . ."

"Alright Tony, thank you so much and may God bless you."

"Goodnight Daddy," Tony said as he walked away.

Few days later, the pastor hurriedly passed to his office through the waiting room where Princess and a co-worker were working.

"Princess!" The Pastor shouted. She quickly went to the office and asked if the Pastor called.

"Are you Princess?" he asked

"No Sir. But there is no Princess here. It's only Mercy and myself"

"Well, Princess is a good name. What if I decide to give you?"

"Daddy, that can't be possible. Princess is a female name."

"By the way, how about your parents?" Pastor asked. She looked down and stood in silence for a while.

"They are dead"

"Sorry James, but haven't you any relation?"

"I have but they are very far and . . ." she paused and crocodile tears dropped from her eyes.

"Sorry Please. Have you ever gone to see them?"

"No Sir." She replied.

"Don't worry James, there is no problem; you can go but call Mercy for me." Princess left the office wondering why the Pastor asked such questions. Anyway, she felt it could be out of sheer concern.

After some weeks, the Pastor invited Tony again.

"Tony,(he began) have you really studied your friend James?"

"How?"

"Well, all this while, I have been furtive in my investigations but I felt there is the need to go along with you. Someone came to inform me that James is not a man."

"What?" Exclaimed Tony standing to his feet.

"Sit down, the Pastor told him. have you ever noticed any sign? Or suspected him at any point?"

"No sir, but . . . I recalled a time I went to the room and met him undressed. He immediately used a towel to cover his body. I only picked my key and left, though I had mixed feelings about why a man would cover himself when a fellow man comes into the room."

'Have you ever seen him undressed?" The Pastor asked

"Eh . . . No! Even during hot seasons he sleeps with his jackets on and that has been his lifestyle."

"I want you to be closer to him than ever. Study him properly and know the truth about him. Avoid suspicious move. Be very careful." So, Tony departed.

When he was coming home, Tony bought meat and pineapple juice on his way home that evening for Princess. On arrival, he saw Princess and Anita in the room.

"Excuse me, husband and wife," said Tony as he entered.

'You're welcome," replied the lesbians.

After greeting, they all ate and drank together. Tony's eyes were wide open and inquisitive yet he noticed nothing more than the usual James he had known. Tony tried all through that week to see if he could get cogent evidence but all his effort was to no avail.

When Tony told the Pastor the failure of his investigation, the Pastor told him not to worry for God would definitely expose her at the right time if she was actually impersonating. So Tony left.

"James, Tony called one night. Do you know what someone said?"

"What?"

"That you are a woman."

"Who said that?" Princess asked.

"They said it's somebody in this compound."

She immediately ran out of bed and stood at the middle of the compound that night and shouted: "Who is that man that said I'm a woman? Let him come out and meet me here and I will show him the difference between a man and a woman."

The occupants all came out of their rooms to see the 'wonders'. Neighbours were equally attracted to the scene. They pleaded with her and she went in. That night marked the beginning of widespread rumour about James' identity. Many had this notion all the while but could not bring it out because of fear of embarrassment should the assertion be proved wrong.

When the Pastor learned about her reaction the previous night, he felt it was time to act fast before it was too late. He invited the elders of his church for an urgent meeting. There he narrated all that Mr. Chike told him and his undercover investigations. They were amazed at the story.

"How could a woman impersonate, stay in the community, associate with people and yet remained unidentified? Could this be really true? If it is true, then could there be spiritual forces behind it?" Some elders asked. "Could the allegation against James be a framed work of some ill-luck wishers playing to the gallery?" Whatever the case is, the truth must be known. So, the elders came to consensus that Princess be called to defend the allegation.

Princess walked into the Pastor's office only to see all the elders waiting for her.

"James!" the Pastor called.

"Yes Sir." Princess answered.

"You are welcome; have a seat. We were told something about you. That's why we have called you to give you a chance to probably clear yourself of it. It is alleged that you are not a man. We have called you here today to say what you have to say about the allegation."

Princess put her head down and began to tell her story.

"I don't know why people like setting me up. For the fact that I have a female voice, does that make me a female? Are there no men that have female structure? Please look at me carefully," she stood up on her feet and turned round.

The elders sat down in amazement.

"Sit down" one of them commanded,

"Why do you have a perforated ear?"

"I did that when I was a sinner but now I have repented."

"It's all right, said the Pastor. We are really sorry for the interrogation. We called you because we are concerned as your spiritual parents. You can now go. There is no problem. Okay?"

The elders decided that the elderly man be called to be at the next sitting where Princess would be called again to come and remove her dress for the elders to settle the controversial issue once and for all. It was on a Sunday evening when the elders reconvened to finalize Princess' case.

"Do you know this man?" the pastor asked princess.

"No," she replied.

"Are you not Princess?" Chike cuts in.

"Look at me carefully. You are the daughter of Mr. Jones my friend. You left home some years ago after a fight at a party, which led to a person's death. The police were after you and you never returned . . ."

"You are a liar!" Princess shouted, standing to her feet.

"Do I look like a woman?" Tears dropped down from her eyes.

The Pastor calmed her down.

"All we want to know is the truth and nothing but the truth. There are seven men and three women. You are a man. All we want you to do is just pull your shirt here in our presence so that everyone here will be convinced beyond reasonable doubt that you are innocent of the allegation and this case will be put to rest." "Is that all you people want? Princess asked. 'Just wait and see."

Knowing so well that if she pull her shirt off the cat would be let out of the bag, Princess stood up, pretending to be undressing her jacket, took some steps towards the door and ran out of the office. The leaders opened their mouths in amazement as they watched. They all rushed to the door but could not see her as she ran to an unknown destination.

The case was reported to the police and the policemen went to Anita's house that evening but met a mighty padlock on the door. The news spread round like wild fire. Everyone was made to be on the alert.

At about twelve midnight, Princess walked into the compound. As soon as she opened the gate, a neighbour saw her and immediately ran to the police. As she opened the door with her own key, Tony jumped out of bed.

"Where are you coming from this night?" Tony asked.

Before the man left to call the police he woke his wife who alerted all other neighbours. As Tony was talking with her, in a jiffy, the whole room was filled with people. Princess turned towards them.

"I know what you people want to know. That I am not a man. Yes, I want to tell you all today that I'm not James. My real name is Princess and I'm a lady. You have known, right? Do your worst."

"So I have been living with a lady all this while?" Tony said to himself.

"Yes and what about it?" Princess said, picked her bag.

"You will not go out of this room today," Tony said.

"You are a devil. Please someone should call the police immediately."

"Police? If you like call a legion of army to come here." Princess immediately picked her bag and wanted to run out but the people blocked the way. She made some karate gesture and yells to make the people give way but before she started displaying her skills the policemen arrived. Two of them paved their way into the room.

"Stop or I shoot," one of the policemen warned.

Princess stopped, looking at the gun in the policeman's hands.

"Hands up!" if you move, I will shoot you."

The policeman arrested and handcuffed Princess and she was taken away.

So she came to the end of the road at about midnight that fateful Sunday.

CHAPTER EIGHT

THE NEW LIFE

Princess sat down quietly in her new abode, the police cell, as she reminisced. "Could this be the end of the road? What will all and sundry say? Would I be able to live in any part of this world again? What about those I outsmarted? Would they ever forgive me? Does it mean that I will go to jail? For how long? I am in trouble! Why was I born in the first place? Would it not have been better if my mother had not conceived me or better still, if she had aborted me. Would anything good ever come out of me again? Well, let the worse happen" She concluded.

The cell was a small room with iron bars. It has little holes that allow in air for ventilation that was shared by inmates. In the cell, it was hard to know when it is night and when it is day, but for slight rays of morning sunrise. The cell served as the living room as well as the bedroom, at the same time the toilet. Its inhabitants consist not only of humans but other living organisms such as bedbugs, mosquitoes, and flies. The humble abode has neither mattress nor bed for its inhabitants. The most comfortable bedding was the rough floor, which the occupants scrambled for. The stench from the 'bucket toilet' alone was sufficient to humble a stubborn gangster.

Princess refused to cooperate with the police during investigations.

"Look at me carefully, one of the police officers said, if you don't want to regret ever being born, you better cooperate with us."

"Are you a man or a woman?" One of the officers asked.

"What can you see?" Princess interrupted. 'Are you seeing a man or a woman?"

After hours of fruitless interrogation, one of the officers suggested that Princess should pull off her shirt. She out-rightly refused. After a fierce battle, the officers decided to apply force. Knowing well that there was no way of escape for her, Princess, agreed to cooperate.

"Now tell us, are you a man or woman?"

"I am a woman," Princess said.

"Jesus Christ!" The two police officers shouted simultaneously. There was sudden silence immediately at her answer. They gazed at her in amazement as tears rolled down her eyes.

"Now you have to do one more thing to convince all of us. Pull off your shirt."

Princess pulled the first shirt which was almost wet with tears.

"Pull the T-shirt," one of the officers commended.

Princess reluctantly pulled off the T-shirt.

"Take off the bra top and girdle."

Princess finally pulled her clothes and stood before the officers, a young woman with a well-built man structure. While crying profusely, Princess confessed to the police how Anita made her to impersonate.

"Do you know that whosoever falsely impersonates another, whether that other is real or fictitious, commits an offence?" One of the officers asked.

"Yes." She nodded.

All attempt to get Anita arrested proved abortive as she took to her heels immediately she learnt of Princess' arrest.

Princess was charged to court for impersonation and she pleaded guilty to the charge. A lawyer who was moved by her story represented her *'pro bono'*. He made a plea of allocotus on her behalf, praying the court to temper justice with mercy since the accused admitted committing the offence thereby saving the precious time of the court. He further informed the court that pleading guilty to the said offence is an indication of true repentance and the accused has learned her lessons and that she has promised not to repeat such act again.

However, Princess was convicted and sentenced to three years imprisonment without an option of a fine. So Princess was taken into the prison.

The walls of the prison were so high that no sane human being would ever dream of escaping from there. Princess looked at it from an angle of elevation as tears rolled down her eyes. She was handed over to the prison authorities who registered her name and welcomed her to the new three-year-free abode.

Princess cried all through her first day in prison and a concerned inmate went to her.

"Hello friend, why are you crying?" the lady asked.

Princess gazed at her without a word.

"My sister," the Lady continued. "Listen to me. Many persons in this prison are not criminals. They are merely scapegoats but I was a criminal. I joined a gang of robbers in the college and we were caught during one of our operations. And in the case of my sister, Rose, she was implicated in a theft case which led to her conviction. She is innocent. Sister . . . , the Lady continued changing posture . . . . being in prison is not the end of life for you. You have so many things to learn here and you can still fulfill your purpose in life after your jail term. After all, many have left prison to become presidents of respectable countries. You must stop crying and think of possible ways of amending your ways if you have done something wrong. We are not afraid or ashamed to discuss our past because we are now new creatures. We have resolved to forget about the past and look forward to the future. Thank God for salvation. Make up your mind to forget the past and focus on your future."

"Thank you," Princess said as the lady walked away.

Early in the morning the next day, while Princess was gazing at others not knowing what to do, the lady walked up to her and said:

"Good morning," sister."

"Good morning," she replied.

"How was your night?"

"Fine."

"I'm sure you didn't spend the whole night thinking."

"No." Princess answered.

"Didn't mosquitoes and bedbugs disturb you?" The lady asked smiling.

"Well, since I slept in the mosquitoes net, I didn't feel anything." Princess answered with a liberal smile.

"What is your name?"

"Princess."

"Are you a king's daughter?"

"Not at all!" Princess said smiling.

"Then why Princess?"

"Well my parents gave that name to me. They said I was beautiful."

"That's a wonderful, nice and beautiful name! You are indeed a Princess."

"Thanks."

"And yours?"

"Grace."

"That's lovely."

"Though that was not my initial name, I changed to Grace in prison when I repented from my past evil ways. Grace means unmerited favour. If not for God's Grace, I would have died long ago in my robbery activities and probably gone to hell, but now I am a changed person in Christ."

"That's good."

"Any way, let's go and perform our morning duties. We shall continue later."

Grace concluded.

Not long after then, Princess and Grace became close cronies. They were always together and doing things in common. One day after lunch, Grace asked Princess a question:

"Are you born again?"

"Born again?" Princess asked.

"Yes" Grace responded.

"What do you mean?" Princess asked.

"Well that's alright . . . but what brought you here?"

(Princess became sober) "It's a long story, I don't really know how and where to start. Anyway, just forget, I will tell you some other time".

"Well that's alright . . . but what Church do you attend?"

"Church?" Princess asked again.

"Yes, I mean where do you fellowship."

"I don't think I have any. When I was with my parents, I used to attend one in the village but since I left home, I haven't gone to church except for a few years ago when I . . . I . . . I . . . mean . . . just forget please."

"Why are you refusing to open up my sister? Confessing your wrongs is a prerequisite for forgiveness. The scripture says if you confess your sins, God is faithful and just to forgive you. Jesus has paid the price for your sins. You have been redeemed by the blood of the lamb. All you need to do is to repent, believe and you will be saved."

Tears rolled down Princess' eyes. She remained silent for a while looking sorrowful.

'Princess, she called, today is the day of salvation. Tomorrow maybe too late; so if you'll make up your mind, it must be now'.

"Grace, can you please leave me alone for a moment?" Princess pleaded.

"Alright, there will be prison fellowship later today, will you come with me?"

"Alright," Princess said.

The prison ministry, being a group of believers who have answered God's call and accepted the great commission to reach out to those in the prison also take the gospel of hope through Christ to many in prison who are dejected, isolated, hopeless, abandoned and neglected.

That evening at the fellowship, God gave a very strong challenge through the speaker. Princess was convicted by the Holy Spirit and she could not resist the move of God. She took a bold step of faith and moved to the altar, knelt down as she wept profusely. She was led to Christ by the minister, after which she narrated her story from the beginning to the end in tears. Other inmates could not withstand it but joined in tears. It was a deliverance and revival service altogether.

After a counselling session with the prison ministers, Princess was given a copy of the Holy bible and Grace became her Bible study mate. Princess became serious with the study of the Word of God. They used most of their leisure periods for Bible study and prayers.

In about a year and half, Princess became strong and dedicated to her new faith. She converted many inmates to Christ. She spent all her time in prison serving God. She changed her name from Princess to Grace. When asked why, she said the name 'Grace' is a special name. Apart from the fact that Grace led her to Christ, the name means unmerited favour. "Since God allowed me all through the years I wasted in sin and He found me worthy to be called among His children, it is a divine unmerited favour and so no name could fit better than Grace."

Princess' new life in prison affected not only her fellow inmates but prison staff. She utilized every opportunity she had to preach to everyone regardless of their status. She faced a lot of persecution as she preached to people; she was mocked several times by those who felt she did not know what she was doing. She was mocked and cajoled in many ways. Princess had physical discouragement and embarrassments at different times. Some alleged that she was disturbing and trying to impose her religion on everybody. The authorities warned her several times but that did not make her give up.

After three years jail term, Princess was released. She wept the day she finally left the prison. She gathered the inmates and gave them her last exhortation in tears.

"I wish I had more time to stay with you but it's certain that to everything there is a season and a time to every purpose under the heaven.

It's time for me to go. However, this shall not be our final parting. I shall come from time to time to visit and have fellowship together with you. Encourage one another and spread the good news of Christ. Pray always and don't give the devil a chance. You are the light and salt of the prison, maintain that saltiness and let the light keep shinning. It shall be well with all of us in Jesus' name." She concluded and the inmates shouted Amen.

Princess now popularly known as Grace was received outside the prison gates by members of the prison ministry, the church Pastor and his wife who had been a source of encouragement to her and many others. The spectators witnessed an impromptu celebration. The highlight of the ten minutes occasion include songs of praise, dancing, weeping (tears of joy) and prayer of thanksgiving. The spectators in company of the celebrant later proceeded to the Pastor's house for the completion of the ceremony.

Three months after Princess was release. The pastor called her and said to her: "I am sure you've rested enough by now . . ."

"Yes Sir." Princess answered.

"So, I think you can start executing your plans now while you await your resumption at school in the next two months."

"Alright sir"

"We will start next week."

"Thank you sir" Princess answered.

At about ten o clock in the morning of that fateful Thursday, Princess and Pastor Ben were at the office of the reverend whom she deceived some years ago. The moment he saw Princess, he shouted 'Jesus' and paused for a while.

'What brought you here again?'

"Sir, Princess said confidently, standing to her feet. I am no longer the former James you used to know. That was fictitious, a name to cover up my atrocities. I am now a new creature. I mean I am born again. I am indeed sorry for all I've done. I have come to ask for your forgiveness. I know it was the schemes of the devil. Though he succeeded in using me, I thank God that I did not die a sinner. I am now a changed person." She said.

"Thank you Jesus, the reverend said. I am really happy that you've realized your mistakes and turned to God finally. You must not give a chance to the devil again. Hold on to your faith and God will see you through!"

"Thank you sir" Princess answered.

After a counseling session, the ministers prayed with her and asked her to come on Sunday to share her testimony with the entire church. Princess told the whole story of her life to the congregation from childhood to prison. As she did so with tears, many wept with her in their sober reflection of the past. She also told the church that she heard the call of God while in prison; so she would by God's grace start her pastoral training soon. The whole church prayed for her and many gave their lives to Christ as a result of her testimony.

In Princess' former compound where she stayed with Tony, people gathered roundabout. She spoke to them about Christ after apologizing over her previous wayward life. She went to the hotel she worked years back to also do the same.

Two weeks later, the Pastor, his wife and Princess left for Princess' village. The twenty-two-hour journey was so hectic that they had to break at certain points to rest and to refresh on arrival. Princess was so spruce as she and the visitors walked into the compound. No one recognized her at first but as soon as a neighbour spotted her, she shouted and there arose a sudden pandemonium. They rushed her, hugged her and scrambled for a talk with her. As soon as Mrs. Jones came out of the house, a fresh wailing ensured. Tears of joy flowed as she ran to meet her prodigal daughter. They hugged each other and wept for quite some time.

"Mummy, I'm sorry," princess said kneeling down.

Without response, her mum held her by the hand and led her to the room. The mother welcomed the visitors and asked a rhetorical question.

"So you are still alive?" the mother said with gladness.

"Yes Mum. Here am I, still alive." Princess answered.

"Thank God you came back alive"

Immediately the news got to Mr. Jones at a neighbour's house. He rushed down home and met a crowd. He walked passed everybody without a word. Just by the entrance, Princess rushed to meet him. He could not resist her sight. He hugged her for a while without a word. He withdrew for some seconds and hugged her again. Tears ran down her chicks as she said:

"Daddy, I've done you wrong. I know that I am not worthy of your forgiveness, but please forgive me for the sake of God."

Mr. Jones could not hold his tears. It flowed freely like rain for the first time in forty-two years. He led her to a seat and kept gazing at her. Friends, neighbours and well-wishers kept coming in to see for themselves the girl whose disappearances remained a mystery to the villagers for many years.

After a moment of tears, Princess introduced Pastor Ben and his wife to her parents and others who were in the room. Princess began to narrate her story from the genesis to the migration, the misery, followed by the impersonation to her fake deliverance which gave birth to the revelation resulting to her new life. Her story ended with tears in everybody's eyes. It was as if a gas was released in the room. Pastor Ben took over from there.

"We are happy that Princess is now a changed person. Today should not be a day of mourning but of joy because Princess served the devil for years. She wasted years in sin yet God's mercy and grace kept her. Now that she is a new creature, behold old things have passed away. She is just like the prodigal son who left home for a long time and returned after realizing his mistakes. The Bible says there was merriment in his father's house. Princess was lost but now found. This surely calls for celebration, thanksgivings and praises to God. Instead of mourning, we should rejoice!"

The following Sunday, Princess went to her church in the village. She told them a short version of her story and apologized to all for what happened some years back.

Princess left the village later for the Bible College. She was dedicated to her studies and service unto the Lord. She became a unique student because winning souls for Christ to her was a top priority. She traveled from city to city, town to town, village to village as well as hamlet to hamlet preaching to save many. She was invited several times for crusades and outreaches to share her experiences and testimonies. She successfully completed her studies at the Bible School and was subsequently ordained.

Her life as a Pastor was so challenging. She was dedicated to her calling and service to God. She suffered many persecutions and trials but she did not look back. The devil used her former friends to sow seeds of discouragement in her but Princess never allowed it to germinate. Some used her past life as a weapon of discouragement but she was sure of one thing; that she is a new creature and that old things have passed away. Princess also knew that since she is born again, the spirit of sin and lesbianism have no power over her.

About a year and two months later, Princess got married to a Pastor. Their union was not only a blessing to their friends and relations but the entire household of God. She lived happily with her husband. She became a role model to other women in the church. She was meek, honest, prudent, gentle, kind, caring, tolerant, neat, obedient, respectful, humble, peaceful, accommodative and submissive. She was indeed a mother to all.

Princess gave birth to three children and she trained them in the way of Lord. Her discipline in the Lord shaped her children so much that her life reflected in them; Annas, Sonia and Banito as they grew up in the fear of the Lord and were obedient, disciplined, self-controlled, respectful and honest. They were a source of blessing not only to their parents but as well to the society.

Anita, Princess' former lesbian lover became frustrated in life because she felt the whole world seemed not to contain her. She was gradually depreciating and dying in silence. No help came from fellow lesbians.

They rather compounded her problem and the whole world seemed not to be of any help. One day, a crusade was to be held in a city. Princess was invited as the guest speaker. It was a great crusade and so there was massive publicity. Anita who did not know Princess' whereabouts since her arrest saw Princess' on the television as the guest speaker of the citywide crusade. "No! This can't be true . . . impossible! Is this not Princess?" She left her seat with her eyes fixed on the television but did not move closer. When the advert was over, she was highly troubled.

"But could this be true? After all, she was arrested and she should be in jail. We were together and I know she can never stop lesbianism. How could she be a Pastor? If that is true then I'll be a Bishop." Anita told herself, and she laughed, making mockery of her imagination.

Two days later, Anita saw the crusade Poster. She stood by it, took a cursory look and tears rolled down her eyes. "It is indeed true. This is Princess! She exclaimed. Now a Pastor? How? When? But look at me. What am I doing? I am getting old, frustrated and with no future. Why can't I look for Princess? I must look for her!" She decided.

Anita was one of the earliest persons to be seated at the crusade ground that evening. She sat in the front row with lots of curiosity and anxiety written on her face. When the speaker arrived, Anita could not help, but she kept looking to be sure she has not mistaken someone else for Princess. When Princess started preaching, Anita began to cry, she wept bitterly.

"If you are here and have not repented from your sin, then you are already dead. I mean you are alive but dead. I was a sinner before. I was an impersonated lesbian, I practiced lesbianism to the core, faked my identity, stole and even killed; I was a drunkard, smoker and a prostitute. There is no evil that I haven't committed but when I met Jesus, everything changed. He took me the way I was, purged me, washed me, cleansed me, forgave all my sins and delivered me from the bondage of sin. I'm now born again; 'am a new creation. I've nothing to do with sin. Today is the day of salvation. If you are in sin like I was, today is your day of salvation."

Before she finished, Anita was already swimming in the pool of her tears. She silently left her seat; walked to the podium, knelt down and kept on weeping. Although Princess did not notice her, she prayed with all who repented and gave their lives to Christ.

After the day's session, Anita sent a short note to Princess. The moment Princess saw the note; she could not wait for a minute. She ran out, hugged Anita and both began to cry. When they got inside, Anita immediately went on her knees and said, "Princess, I'm sorry. Please forgive me." Princess went to her, lifted her up and asked her to sit down.

"I introduced you to lesbianism and made you impersonate but when you were arrested, I ran away. It hasn't been easy for me since then. I felt depressed and frustrated. I lost all the hope in the world. Sometimes I feel like committing suicide. I am sure this crusade was organized for me. I still want you to forgive me; also pray for me again. I'll from now on follow and serve your God."

"Today is my happiest day" Princess said. "It's worth more than a thousand days. Because you have now repented and given your life to Christ, you are now a new creature, old things have passed away. You must not go back to them again. Say goodbye to lesbianism and all sorts of evil. Embrace Jesus Christ and he will definitely see you through."

After two hours of counseling, she prayed for Anita, Anita repented— left lesbianism and she became a dedicated child of God.

Epilogue

Moral decadence among youths can be largely blamed on parental upbringing—from the story of Princess, we can say that is true. She did not get the necessary moral upbringing and she lived a miserable life. Even her teacher while she was in school had sent a letter to her parents at a point to ask them why she put up bad characters and to tell them to give her good home training. That means even teachers can do less if parents do not do their best to bring up their children in the way they should go.

The other reason for moral decadence among youths is bad company. As the good book says, evil communication corrupt good manner. Princess lived her life according to the dictate of her friends who offered her help to hide from her past. The lesson in this book therefore is for both parents and youths; because, parents must take the first responsibility for not bringing up their children the way they should go, and youths must understand that their future is determined by their actions and the kind of friends they keep.